SIX - STRANGE STORIES OF LOVE

AROUND THE WORLD COLLECTION

POORNIMA MANCO

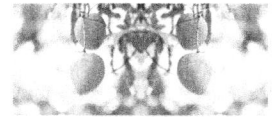

Copyright © 2023 by Poornima Manco

All rights reserved.

No part of this book may be reproduced in any form or by any electronic or mechanical means, including information storage and retrieval systems, without written permission from the author, except for the use of brief quotations in a book review.

Cover designed by MiblArt

For my Family

Time is too slow for those who wait, too swift for those who fear, too long for those who grieve, too short for those who rejoice, but for those who love, time is eternity.
    Henry Van Dyke

CONTENTS

Foreword	ix
1. Hair	1
2. The Fake Rolex	25
3. Karolina	51
4. The Purple Ribbon	75
5. A New Place	96
6. La Dolorosa	113
Afterword	141
Acknowledgments	143
About the Author	145
Also by Poornima Manco	147

FOREWORD

These stories are unconventional. They are not romantic per se, but they are about love. All kinds of love. As a writer, I wanted to explore this emotion in all its depth, variety and complexity.

This is the last book in the *Around the World Collection*, and I have once again taken you, the reader, to different lands and cultures, while trying to show the commonalities between us, and the universality of the human condition.

However, expect the unexpected when you begin. These stories may surprise you. In fact, I hope they do. But I also hope they delight, inform and entertain you.

Don't forget to leave a review that tells me what you thought of these tales. Your reviews make me a better writer.

Happy reading!

HAIR

Amma insisted on oiling my hair daily.

"Coconut oil nourishes the scalp, Divya. It will make your hair grow long and thick, like mine." She would massage the roots of my hair, spreading the sweet, fragrant oil down the length of my locks, before plaiting and decorating them with strands of jasmine flowers.

Her own hair was dark, lustrous, and well past her knees. On the days she washed it, she would lie on a coir mat on the terrace, spreading out her tresses behind her so that the sun and the breeze would dry them naturally. Even so, it would take an hour. This was Amma's time, and we knew not to disturb her. She would lie there with her eyes closed, listening to the songs playing softly on the transistor radio.

Appa would tiptoe around her, sometimes gazing at her in wonderment. She was like an *Apsara*, he had whispered to us once. A beautiful divine creature that had landed in our midst. In his worshipping words, I gleaned just how lucky he found himself to be. Amma was extraordinary. She looked nothing like the women who lived in the houses next to us—small, plump and nondescript. Amma was tall, her skin like milky coffee, her hazel eyes snapping and crackling with an intense energy, her waist still so slender after three children. Appa, on the other hand, was skinny and balding, with a rice belly protruding from under the white shirts he wore with his *mundu*. Appa adored Amma. We all did. She was a woman who wouldn't settle for any less.

In Kerala, women were meant to be the heads of households. Ours was a matrilineal society, unlike most of India. Truth was, men still ran most households. Men who left for work every morning, and when they returned in the evening, expected their dinners to be laid out for them, the house spic and span, and the children out of earshot. In our home, though, Amma was truly the matriarch. Nothing happened without her knowledge or consent. She was a force of nature, a woman so determined and fierce that even the most macho men quaked in her presence. Yet, it did not stop them from comparing their own insipid wives to her.

Appa knew that when his late parents had arranged a match with Amma, he had struck gold. He showered her with saris and jewels. He took her on long holidays to the tea estates of Munnar, leaving us in the care of his elderly aunt. We didn't mind. Those were the only days we could run wild with no real supervision. In a way, it was a holiday for us too.

I was the eldest of three. My two brothers were three and five years younger, and at fourteen, in Amma and Appa's absence, I was the one they turned to for guidance. Playing mother suited me fine. I would assume Amma's imperious tone while ordering them to wait hand and foot on me, giggling as their little legs ran to fetch and carry.

Then in the evenings, I would read them scary stories from my English storybook while Valiya Ammayi, Appa's spinster aunt, watched perplexed as they shivered in terror. At night, one of them would wet the bed and the other cry out for Amma, while I slept blissfully unaware until the next morning. When Amma would return to all the complaints, I'd plead ignorance only for her to take me aside, give me a tight slap on my bottom, then forgive me almost immediately.

What none of the men in the household knew or suspected was

just how soft Amma was on the inside. Her imperious manner was just for show. In reality, she was as soft as a summer mango, all firm flesh and sweetness. Growing up in a house full of men and no mother, she had learned to assert herself early on. But in the Mills and Boon books that she read avidly, in the way she gulped down her sobs at the end of sad movies, and in her kindness towards stray dogs and beleaguered wives, she gave herself away to the women in her vicinity. We knew what she was about, and we loved her even more than the men who were dazzled by her.

I wish I'd thought to ask her more about her own dreams and desires, instead of assuming that she was just there to facilitate mine. She was only a young woman when she had married Appa and settled into domesticity. As a bright child, academic and talented, she could have made so much more of her life than just being someone's wife. Maybe that's why she insisted that I concentrate on my studies and make something of mine. Her thwarted ambitions unknowingly became my template for success.

Still, in her little sphere of influence—her family, her community, her circle of friends—she was indisputably the queen. No one challenged her authority or questioned her wisdom. We rightly assumed that all her decisions would benefit us, and they did. Even her tiny imperfections—an incandescent rage that would overtake her sometimes, or her tendency to disappear into her books at the cost of housework—added to her charm. She wasn't perfect, but she was the closest thing to it and the rest of us basked in her glow, acutely aware, just as Appa was, that we were lucky to have her.

One decision changed everything for us. One decision that came from a place of kindness, of largesse, destroyed all that was beautiful and perfect in our lives. If only I could go back in time and change that fateful day, but I can't. All I can do is record it all for posterity, so that no one ever takes life and its bounty for granted ever again.

It was a Tuesday evening, and I had just woken up from my afternoon nap. Something felt strange. There were storm clouds in the sky, and as I lingered in bed watching them approach through the open windows of my room, the air felt heavy and oppressive. The boys were still asleep next to me, so I straightened the sheet on their little bodies and swung my legs out of bed.

After splashing my face with water and smoothing down my hair, I went in search of Amma. This was the time she would be curled up in her favourite spot near the window with a book in her hands. I wouldn't say a word, just lie down next to her, and her hand would stroke my forehead absently as she remained absorbed in the story. This was our special time when men did not intrude, when words were not needed between mother and daughter, when stillness and silence mingled with unspoken love. I cherished that time. To this day, I can close my eyes and recall the feel of her hands on my skin.

But that evening, she was nowhere to be found. I looked through all the rooms for her, then heard hushed voices out on the verandah and hurried over to see what had upset our evening routine, before stopping short of the door. The word "death" spoken in Appa's gravelly voice halted my feet.

"How did it happen, Etta?" Amma's voice was low, subdued.

"Heart attack, Malathi. He was so overweight that the doctor had told him he must lose 20 kilos or he would be at risk, but he never listened. And Baby fed him too much."

"So sad, no? When are you leaving for the cremation?"

"Rajan has booked the tickets for this evening only. Bus will leave at 10 p.m. I will come back next week after all the formalities are completed."

"Do you want me to come with you?"

"No, no. The children need you here. I will sort it all out, then return."

"And Baby?"

There was silence for a while. I could see Appa's brow furrow as I watched them covertly from the opening in the door.

"Maybe I will bring her back with me. Is that alright?"

"Of course it is! She is your sister and now a young widow. We must help her. I insist you bring her back with you."

"But Malathi, she is difficult, you know. Not having children has made her... uhhh... difficult..."

"Nonsense, Etta! Our children are like her children. She will be fine. I know she treated her husband like an infant, but now she will have actual children she can focus on. It will distract her from her grief. I tell you, it is the only solution."

I shuffled back from the door as Appa rose, and raced back to my room before they discovered I'd been eavesdropping, wondering what all of it meant. We had visited Baby Aunty and her husband in Kochi many years ago, and all I could remember of that time was the many sweets she had fed us. Maybe it would be good to have someone like that in the house. Amma rarely allowed us sugary treats, and I loved sweetmeats.

Appa left later that night after eating a small plate of rice with *sambar* and *papadum*. He seemed to have lost his appetite, but my brothers more than made up for it, eating larger portions than usual. Amma was left to explain where Appa was going and why.

"So, Baby Aunty's husband... you remember Harihar Uncle?" Amma asked, a serious look on her face. The boys shook their heads while I nodded. They were too little to remember our visit, but I already knew what was coming and tried making it easier for Amma.

"Harihar Uncle died this morning from a heart attack. Appa needs to help his sister in Kochi, so he will be there for the next few days. When Baby Aunty comes back with Appa, I don't want you bothering her, okay? She will be very sad, and she will need our help to get better."

The boys looked confused for a minute. Death was only a word to them. They had no real idea what it meant. I had seen what it had done to Radha, my oldest friend, when her mother died unexpectedly six months ago. From being a carefree, high-spirited girl, she had to step up to being the woman of the household. Every ounce of joy and laughter had disappeared from her life, and bit by bit, the girl I had known disappeared too. Death made people invisible. Would Baby

Aunty, the large and loud woman that I remembered, also shrink into nothing after Harihar Uncle's passing?

As Amma combed my hair before school the next morning, weaving the strands into a five-fingered fishtail braid, I asked her, "Is Harihar Uncle in Heaven now?"

Her hands paused for a beat before resuming their work.

"We don't believe in Heaven, Divya."

"Then?"

"If he's lucky, he will be released from the cycle of life, death, and rebirth. If not, he will be reborn in another form. Another body."

"Could he be a woman the next time?"

"He could. Or he could be an animal, even. His Karma from this life will determine his birth in the next one."

Harihar Uncle, with his black bushy beard, the rolls of fat that wobbled under his vest, and his way of snorting before tucking into his food, had always reminded me of a wild boar. That, I decided in my mind, was what he was likely to be born as.

"Will Baby Aunty be living with us now?"

"For a little while, until she decides what she wants to do next."

Amma was so placid as she said this, her kindness and belief that she was doing the right thing so absolute that it calmed me into acceptance too.

How could any of us have foreseen that this was the calm before the storm?

Baby Aunty had not shrunk at all like I'd expected. She had grown even larger than the last time I had seen her at a relative's wedding in Thiruvananthapuram. I had giggled then as she had taken up most of the room on the sofa, the lady sitting next to her almost falling off the other end. Amma had chided me gently, telling me not to make fun of people's weight.

Now, I observed her hauling herself out of the taxi and wondered how she could be younger than Amma. She huffed and puffed while getting out, and as she bent to straighten her sari pleats, I spotted a bald patch on her head. When she looked up, her eyes looked puffy, as if she'd been crying all night.

"Baby!" Amma reached out and embraced her. "Come, come. I've made some coffee for you."

As they passed us standing in the doorway, I smelt something sour on her, like curdled milk. Appa got the cases out of the trunk and paid the taxi driver. I picked up her valise, and the boys carried her plastic hand basket inside. Appa looked tired. He'd been away for nearly ten days, and the snippets of conversations I'd heard between Amma and Valiya Ammayi always revolved around him sorting out inheritance and property. Nothing I could make sense of.

Baby Aunty was sitting on the two-seater sofa while Amma, Appa, and Valiya Ammayi sat squashed together on the small three-seater opposite her. A steaming cup of coffee and a plate of hot *pakoras* were placed in front of Baby Aunty, and every so often her hand would reach over to put a *pakora* in her mouth. She chewed slowly, saying very little, while Appa spoke in fits and starts.

"... the loan was so large... Baby didn't know... had to arrange a sale... Hari never said..."

"So, the poor girl has nothing to her name?" Valiya Ammayi asked, clutching at her gold chain. Baby Aunty was still a 'girl' to her.

"Only a few trinkets and his old Ambassador car." Appa looked upset. Baby Aunty picked up the steel tumbler, blew on the coffee, then swallowed it in one gulp.

"You don't worry, Baby," Amma said, "you'll always have a home with us."

At this pronouncement, Baby Aunty looked at Amma and let out an enormous belch.

Later that night, I asked Amma why she hadn't spoken to any of us children. The boys didn't care, but I did. She had ignored us as if we didn't exist.

"No, *molé*, don't misunderstand her. She is just in shock, that is all. Her entire life has turned upside down. Everything she knew or took for granted has gone. We need to give her a lot of love and understanding. We need to make her feel like a part of our family now, so that she doesn't miss her home too much."

I snuggled into Amma, inhaling her sweet jasmine smell, wondering why making Baby Aunty a part of our family suddenly seemed less appealing.

Perhaps my resentment of her stemmed from my having to give up my room and move in with the boys.

"It's only temporary, Divya," Amma murmured while helping me place my clothes in the boys' armoire.

The boys were excited that I was moving in with them, wanting me to sleep in the middle and read them stories every night; happy to run errands for me. But tormenting them didn't give me joy any longer. My mind was preoccupied by this interloper who looked as if she were setting down very heavy roots in our home. Thick, gnarled, twisty roots that spread underneath the earth, sucking all the sustenance away from the other plants that tried flourishing above.

I never saw Baby Aunty cry. Not once. Not since she'd gotten out of the taxi with swollen eyes. Nor did I hear her speak of her husband again. It was as if he had never existed.

When Amma tried talking to her, she would look at her blankly, then go back to watching the television, as if hypnotised by the activities of the people on the screen.

"I worry about her, Etta. This is not normal. She needs to talk; to vent if need be. She is suppressing her feelings, and it isn't healthy."

"I agree. I've tried talking to her, too. She just doesn't want to address it yet. It's best to leave her be until she is ready. It must have come as an enormous shock to discover that Hari had re-mortgaged the house…"

"… everything that she took for granted has disappeared. It's so sad…"

"It is. But we can set her up again. We have that small property near Thrissur. I was thinking she could live there once she has somewhat recovered."

"It's too early for that, Etta. She needs us right now. Let us give her the love and support she requires. Maybe, in the future, she will be open to relocating?"

I used snippets of conversation to build a picture of the gargantuan woman who sat on our sofa and ate all our snacks. Who looked at us, but didn't see us. Who slept late every morning and went to bed much after the rest of the household had retired.

What went on behind those beady eyes? Those eyes that followed Amma when Amma wasn't aware, smoothing down scanty strands of hair over her bald patch as she watched Amma twist her thick locks into a knot at her nape.

I didn't think she would relocate. She barely stepped out of the house onto the verandah, and rarely did she climb the stairs to the terrace. Her only movement was from the bed to the sofa and back again. Yet she filled every room with her presence. Her dark, brooding malevolence—although I would have been hard pressed to have described it that way back then. But where my language was lacking, my instincts were unerring.

Sympathy has an expiration date, as I discovered in due course. Appa was the first to crack. Baby Aunty had taken over the living room, which used to be his domain. He could no longer watch the news because that interfered with her television programmes, nor could he put on the radio in the morning as that interfered with her sleep.

The boys didn't bother to hide their revulsion for her. She was "an ugly witch" for them, a *mantravādi*. She ate all their snacks; she sat in the toilet for hours when they needed to go desperately, and her beady eyes followed all their movements but barely registered them as little people with needs and wants of their own. They were not vocal in their dislike, but they didn't have the skills to dissemble either, and so everyone knew.

Nearly six months later, even Amma's patience was wearing thin. Baby Aunty had slowly encroached upon everything that Amma found pleasure in. Her Mills & Boon books would regularly disappear, only to be found dog-eared and food-encrusted in Baby Aunty's possession. Her regular evening chats with the neighbourhood ladies had all but come to a halt because Baby Aunty would hover near them, belching and letting out gas, putting them all off. One time she had even borrowed Amma's favourite sari and torn the hem while hauling herself out of the sofa.

As for me, I had never liked or trusted her. From my childish dislike, something more concrete had emerged. I watched her as she watched Amma, instinctively picking up on her jealousy and her simmering resentment for the tall, striking woman who had given her shelter in her home.

Yes, Amma could inspire envy just by being who she was. But Baby Aunty's ill-will stemmed from something else. In my very limited knowledge of the world, of the dynamics between men and women, but particularly between women, I would have said that she begrudged Amma her hair.

I had seen how she watched Amma oil her hair and comb it, how she licked her lips every time a few strands fell to the floor. I'd even come upon her collecting those strands before anyone could sweep them away.

"What are you doing, Baby Aunty?" I'd asked, curious to see her knotting the hair into a little ball and tucking it into her sari *pallav*.

"Nothing." She'd glared at me before waddling back to her room (*my* room) and shutting the door.

Maybe I should have told Amma then, but what could I have said? My unease came from something indefinable and amorphous.

Baby Aunty had refused all offers of relocation, bursting into tears anytime anyone tried talking of the future. Her only ally in the house was Valiya Ammayi, who had lived the lonely life of a spinster and sympathised with Baby Aunty's plight as an impoverished widow.

"She is all alone in the world except for us. How can you expect her to live by herself in Thrissur? What will she do there? Who will she talk to?"

"She barely talks to us," Appa protested, looking to Amma for support.

At first, Amma had taken care of Baby Aunty as if she were another child in the house. But in the last few months, she had started to chafe at the ingratitude and lethargy that Baby Aunty displayed towards us. There had been many conversations that mentioned "our children" and "our duty" in angry whispers that even I could decipher.

"I think it is time," Amma declared, her voice stern. "We have done all that we could. Baby must take charge of her own life moving forward." She looked at Valiya Ammayi and softened her tone. "You can join her if you like."

Our wrinkled old aunt straightened up and said, "I am happy here. I do not wish to move."

Amma flung her long, thick plait over her shoulder and said, "Then it's settled. We will take Baby to Thrissur next month. We can hire a cook and cleaner to help her in the house. In time, I'm sure she will make friends and be grateful for the independence."

I had been listening in on their conversation from my little nook in the corner, and was best placed to see Baby Aunty standing at the door to my bedroom, her mouth moving convulsively as she too eavesdropped on a conference that she had been excluded from. I felt sorry for her then. It was her future, after all. But she had displayed so little interest in it, it was no wonder that others were deciding for her. Something that I vowed to myself I would never allow to happen to me.

At that moment, though, her expression changed. Her features hardened as she stared at the back of Amma's head. Her small eyes narrowed and her lips pursed into a thin line. Even from where I was sitting, I could detect the rage that radiated off her. She stood there for a moment, her large frame quivering before she slunk back into the room, shutting the door quietly.

There was never a showdown between Amma and Baby Aunty that precipitated the decision. Just one incident where Amma lost her temper, and the seeds of what was to follow were sowed then.

It was a Sunday afternoon. Amma's ritual of washing her hair and lying on the coir mat was practically sacrosanct in our household. Except that when she unrolled her mat, there were several large black carpenter ants that crawled out. Hundreds and hundreds of them.

Amma recoiled, throwing the mat aside before spotting a large brown stain on it. A coffee spill. Sweet coffee loaded with teaspoons full of sugar. Baby Aunty's coffee.

"Baby!" she bellowed, but no one showed.

She raced downstairs, her wet hair leaving a trail of water droplets on the stairs. I followed her, motioning to the boys to stay on the terrace.

"Did you spill coffee on my mat, Baby?" Amma stood at the door to my room while Baby Aunty remained lying in bed. I could see that even she was frightened by Amma's temper. She shook her head up and down, mute, her triple chins wobbling.

"Never EVER touch my stuff again without asking me first. Okay?"

Baby Aunty nodded quickly, and as Amma turned and stomped off, I saw the fear replaced by something else. What was it? Glee? Anger? Or the more insidious resolve to avenge herself against a woman who was everything that she wasn't?

Amma was never ill, so when she got sick it came as a shock to us. It started with a sore throat and none of us could have foreseen where it would end.

"Etta, it is probably the tamarind I ate yesterday. Stop fussing!"

Appa continued to bring Amma cups of tea, insisting that she stay in bed as she looked exhausted. Amma fought back.

"I am not an invalid! What is this? How will the household run if I am not managing it?"

"Malathi, you need to rest. Your voice…"

"Is hoarse, that is all. I have stayed in bed long enough. Divya, you keep an eye on the boys while I prepare the dinner."

When Amma made up her mind, it was impossible to change it.

I sat on the top step of our porch, half-watching the boys play out on the street with their friends while completing my homework. Amma was in the kitchen and Appa had gone to the shops to buy mutton for the *pepper varattu* she wanted to prepare for dinner. The air was still and heavy; the only voices were of the boys screaming as they scored runs in their game of cricket. I bent over the world map in my geography book, examining the outlines of all the continents; fascinated by the thought of people who spoke, ate, dressed and worked differently from us. I wanted to visit these countries, eat their foods, learn their languages, and explore their lands. But how? Amma had said that education would take me far. How far? And could I bear to leave my dear family behind?

Just then, a thin, reedy voice emerged from a window. It was singing a lullaby. Tuneless, wavering on the higher notes, it was not a voice that I recognised. Drawn from my station on the step, I followed it to its source, peering cautiously through the window it was coming from.

Baby Aunty was sitting on the bed, facing sideways, playing with a doll on her lap. With a needle and thread, she seemed to sew something onto the scalp as she sang, *"Rari Rariram Raro…"* Her hand cradled the cloth doll's head as if it were a baby, and as I watched her, I realised that the black thread she was using was Amma's hair! An involuntary gasp escaped me and I ducked just as she swung around, halting her song.

When she came out to investigate, I was back on the porch and immersed in my homework, calling out to the boys occasionally to be careful with the ball.

"Don't hit the window!" I cried out, pretending I hadn't seen her as she crept up on me.

"What are you doing?" This was the first time she had spoken to me in six months, and I looked up at her open-mouthed.

"I... I'm doing my homework," I stuttered.

"Hmm." She looked at the book in my hand, then at the boys playing on the street before padding back indoors.

Valiya Ammayi had cautioned me years ago when I cut my nails or combed my hair, to always make sure that I disposed of the remains carefully.

"But why?" I'd asked, curious as she picked up bits of my nail clippings from the porch where I'd cut them.

"In my village, a young woman was lured away by a man who had collected all her nail and hair droppings. He used them to put a spell on her. Black magic, child!" Valiya Ammayi's eyes had bulged as she spoke. "Never, ever let your hair or nails fall into anyone's grasp. You do not know what their motives may be."

Now, I wondered why Baby Aunty had been collecting Amma's hair. Why was she using it for the doll? Was she casting a spell on Amma? I needed to ask Valiya Ammayi right away.

Calling out to the boys not to wander far, I went in search of Valiya Ammayi. She was sitting on the ledge of the terrace wall, cracking her betel nuts as usual. She didn't seem surprised to see me patting the space next to her, indicating I should sit there.

"What is bothering you, Divya?"

"It's... I... you remember how you told me about black magic? About how people use hair and nails to do wicked things?"

She nodded, popping a nut into her mouth and chewing on it slowly.

"I saw Baby Aunty with Amma's hair..."

Valiya Ammayi paused all movement and stared at me.

"What are you saying, child?"

"I... I don't know..." I cried out, still confused about what I'd witnessed, spilling the entire scene out in a gush of words.

Valiya Ammayi set the nutcracker aside and took my hands in hers.

"Divya, this is your aunt. She is a widow who is still mourning her husband. Why would she want to harm Malathi?"

"Maybe because Amma wants her to leave now?"

"Nonsense! Baby doesn't have a wicked bone in her body. She has always been the sweetest, most compliant girl. All this is in your imagination. Now, shoo! Go look after the boys like your mother said."

She picked up the nutcracker and carried on as if I hadn't interrupted her at all.

"You won't tell her, will you?"

"Tell who what?" Valiya Ammayi's eyes bored into me.

"Nothing."

I walked away, unconvinced. I had seen what I had seen. If Baby Aunty wanted to sew hair on her doll's head, why not use thread? Why Amma's hair?

Something was very wrong, and I was determined to get to the bottom of it.

Amma's decline occurred so quickly that all other thoughts and plans fled in the fear and uncertainty of that time. A healthy and robust woman—cooking, talking, reading, laughing one minute—she was in bed the next, coughing and spitting up blood.

Doctors came and went. Appa took her to different hospitals while we waited to hear when they would return and how Amma would recover.

When momentous things happen, children get forgotten. No one explained what was happening. I gathered whatever little I could by listening in to hushed conversations or sneaking in to sit by Amma when Appa was out.

She barely spoke, her face was leached of colour, and there were dark circles under the eyes she kept closed to the world. Her face was animated only when she coughed, twisting in pain at the effort. In the course of a few weeks, her body had shrunk, all dynamic energy ripped from it as she lay there, weak and apathetic. Who was this? This woman didn't seem like Amma at all.

I tried consoling the boys, who were terrified by the turn of events, by telling them that all would be well, that Amma was only temporarily sick. That if they didn't study hard or played too much cricket, she would smack their bottoms as she had always done. But I was terrified too.

It was at this time that Baby Aunty emerged from her torpor. Suddenly, all her lethargy was banished, and she was there in the thick of it, taking over the household and Amma's kitchen; managing our lives while Appa ran around looking for cures and panaceas for his ailing wife.

Suddenly it wasn't just the roots spreading beneath the earth but also the branches of this enormous tree that I still saw Baby Aunty as, that seemed to cover us from every angle.

Valiya Ammayi told me to be grateful.

"I am too old," she said, chewing thoughtfully on her betel nuts. "Baby is good to take charge. Otherwise, who would do all this?"

All this.

Amma's loving but chaotic care of us and her home was replaced by a brisk, emotionless efficiency. A drill sergeant emerged from the hitherto somnambulant woman—one who was almost too eager to take over, to usurp, to dethrone.

Perhaps the most traumatic side effect of Amma's illness was the loss of her hair. That thick, long, glorious mane disappeared almost overnight, her hair falling out in clumps.

"It's the medicine," Valiya Ammayi explained, sorrow etched on her wrinkled visage.

Amma started to resemble a cadaver with the bare minimum of life signs to signal that she was still alive—her shallow breathing, the fingers that would move involuntarily as she slept, her shuffle to the toilet leaning on Appa, before that too became impossible.

How quickly all of it happened! Or maybe that's how it felt to me back then.

Where had my Amma gone? That vibrant woman who could light up any room she walked into? The mother who loved us ferociously, who slipped into a daydream before snapping back to reality with a grin, was slipping out of the very grasp of life now.

"What is wrong with Amma, *Chechi?*" the boys would ask me, refusing to accept my bald-faced lies any longer.

I would shake my head, too scared to vocalise the thought that dominated all our waking hours. Amma was being eaten alive from the inside.

A nebulous thought took hold of me. This was Baby Aunty's doing. She alone had caused Amma to fall sick. It was the black magic she had used that had created the tumour within my mother's body. I knew no one would believe me. Valiya Ammayi was too fond of her, Appa too preoccupied, the boys too young. Only Amma would have listened. She may even have scoffed, but she would have listened.

When it became clear that none of the treatments were working, an old friend of Appa's, a Mr Khayyam, counselled him, *"Dawa nahin, dua zaroori hai."*

Prayers.

I had prayed daily to the pantheon of gods that populated the small shelf in our kitchen. From Shiva to Ganesh, Lakshmi to Durga, Christ to Allah, none had been spared my desperate supplications. All to no avail. Yet, I still believed. Only God—any God, whichever God—could vanquish this disease that was destroying our beloved Amma; could nullify the effects of the spell.

Appa started talking about pilgrimages. Guruvayoor and Sabarimala, Tirupati and Puttaparthi, were all mentioned in the same breath, as his eyes beseeched his aunt and sister for guidance.

"There is the distance and the cost," Appa sat at the table, clasping and unclasping his hands, "but that means nothing, if Malathi can recover."

"You cannot go alone," Valiya Ammayi interjected. "Can Khayyam not go with you?"

"To a temple?" Appa's forehead creased even as Baby Aunty let out a guffaw.

"Oh," Valiya Ammayi's face fell. "Muslim man won't be allowed."

"Will you come?" Appa asked Baby Aunty.

"Then who will run the house and take care of the children?" she squeaked back.

"Where are you planning to go, anyway?" Valiya Ammayi wiped the sweat off her brow with the edge of her sari.

"I think it has to be Tirupati."

"Why there?"

"Vijay from work vouches that Balaji grants your prayers almost instantaneously."

"I'll come." I surprised everyone by entering the room, their faces turning towards me at the same time.

"Divya, you are too…"

Whatever Appa was about to say was cut off by Valiya Ammayi's hand on his forearm.

"Let her come."

Appa bent his head in acknowledgement.

Internally, I vowed I would do whatever it took to bring Amma back to us, even if it meant bargaining with God to take another in her place.

"Don't go," Amma clutched my hand, lucid for the first time in days. Her whispered plea reached inside of me and twisted my heart. We both wept as I hugged her. How could I not go? This was my Amma, and I would walk barefoot on hot coals till the ends of the earth for her.

"Etta…"

Appa rushed to her side.

I turned away from their embrace, shunting the boys outside to allow them to have their moment of privacy.

Valiya Ammayi and Baby Aunty stood next to our packed cases, waiting.

"You will take care of her?" I asked Valiya Ammayi, ignoring Baby Aunty.

"Of course, child. Why else am I here?" She patted my head. "You take care of your Appa, and make sure he eats and rests well. Malathi will recover, I guarantee it."

Her voice was so full of conviction that I allowed it to briefly pacify my fears. It was only then that I turned to Baby Aunty, out of sheer politeness, to say goodbye. Her eyes were guarded, her mouth pursed, and her pat on my arm perfunctory. This woman had no affection for any of us. A shiver went through me and I almost changed my mind then.

The boys came and clung to me, their little bodies trembling with fear.

I kneeled down and hugged them, unable to stem the tears that flowed from my eyes.

"It will be alright, you wait and see. Appa said that Balaji grants all pilgrims their wishes. He will grant ours, too."

"Will Amma get better?"

"Will she walk again?"

"Will her hair grow back, *Chechi*?"

Their questions pummelled me, and I looked up as Appa emerged from the room, hoping he would provide the answers that I couldn't. But he stood there, helpless and defeated, even before we had begun our journey.

"Amma will get better, and yes, she will walk again. As for her hair, it will grow even thicker, longer, and more lush than before." I said this with a resolve I didn't feel, but it calmed them, and that mattered in the moment.

It was nearly 7 p.m. when we left for the train station. The journey was an overnight one. All night, as we rocked in our sleeper berths, I incanted prayers for Amma's recovery. I knew Appa was doing the same.

There is little I remember of the rest of the journey. Everything was a blur of heat and crowds, fatigue and long lines. Appa grasped my hand as we snaked through the pilgrims, depositing our luggage in a small guest house, taking a half hour to wash up before heading towards the temples.

We put on our brave faces for each other, hoping that neither would sense the fear or the desperation that simmered beneath. But here, in this holiest of holy places, we were surrounded by fear and desperation. People had come from all corners of the country to beg Lord Venkateswara to grant them their wishes. Whether that was health or financial well-being, a child or a house, there was a sense of urgency to the prayers, a feeling that time was running out. Or was that all in my imagination?

"I will shave my head," Appa murmured to me.

"What?" I thought I'd misheard him; had concocted this bizarre statement.

"If I give my hair to God, he will forgive me all my sins, and return Malathi to her good health."

I looked at the scanty hair on Appa's head. He was practically bald.

"I want to do the same."

Appa flinched.

"No, Divya! You are a young girl. How can you?"

"My hair is long and thick, like Amma's. Balaji will like it more."

Appa's eyes rested on the plait I had woven clumsily in the guest house, and he sighed.

"If you are sure…?"

"Yes, I am."

Tonsuring of the hair was a simple but lengthy procedure. We had to first procure the blades from the temple authorities. To do this, we joined another queue at Tirumala Tirupati Kalyana Katta. After two hours of queueing, we got to the temple barbers who took the blades and proceeded to shave Appa's hair, and then mine.

As I saw my locks fall to the ground, I wondered if it was enough. Would Lord Venkateswara approve of the sacrifice? Would it wipe clean the evil eye cast by Baby Aunty?

Back at the guest house, we bathed and changed into new clothes. I felt the smoothness of my scalp and examined the shape of my head in the small mirror in the bathroom. I remained dry-eyed. This was for

Amma. Someday, when my hair grew back, I would lie on the terrace with her and recount this strange episode as we listened to the transistor radio in the background.

We finally got our *darshan* the next morning. After hours of queuing, of being pushed and shoved, we had ten seconds to get a glimpse of the deity before they chivvied us along. In those ten seconds, I finally said the words: "Please God, take Baby Aunty instead. Spare my Amma. Please, Balaji!"

Four days later, weary from the journey but filled with optimism, we returned home. Bald-headed, carrying the *prasadam* from Tirupati and overflowing with the beneficence granted by Lord Venkateswara, we returned, certain that Amma would most definitely turn a corner now.

Amma had died the previous night. The night that we had finally slept in our train berths on the journey home, rocked into a deep exhausted slumber, convinced that all would be well, that Balaji would answer our prayers, he had slipped into our home and taken her away forever.

I never believed in god again.

❧

"You seriously believe your aunt killed your mother?" Daisy asks while taking a sip of her wine. The sun is glinting on her blonde mane, turning it golden, surrounding her with a gilded halo.

"Yes," I nod in response, watching as her eyebrows arch in surprise.

The smell of marijuana clings to our hair and clothes. Walking through the streets of New York can do that to you, although maybe Daisy is back to smoking pot again.

"But why?"

"Jealousy." I remember the look in Baby Aunty's eyes and shiver. The woman who finally took over our household after despatching my mother to an early cremation.

"Divya, your mother had stage 4 laryngeal cancer. You've told me so before. Why this sudden volte face?"

"I've told you what the doctors told us, not what I believed. Today, I've told you the truth."

She squints at me as if seeing me for the first time.

"And the hair?"

"Whose hair?"

"Everyone's. Yours, your father's, your aunt's?"

"What a strange question!" I look at her anew. Maybe she isn't that dissimilar to me.

"Appa's grew back in patches. Baby Aunty took to wearing a wig," I shudder in recollection, "and I never let mine grow beyond this length."

She looks at my closely cropped hair and nods.

"Because you were afraid…"

"No," I say, annoyed once again, "because it would have been a betrayal of her. Of Amma. Of everything she was, of her memories."

"I see." She takes another sip of her wine as she contemplates the horizon. The sun is setting over the Hudson, casting an orange glow on the water. The skyscrapers reflect the light back, opaque and silent in their majesty, unyielding before the might of the celestial body.

Sometimes I miss the verdant playground of my youth, the heavy monsoons, the smell of vetiver, the soothing sounds of nature, the warm, earthy clasp of my motherland.

Only sometimes.

"Why have you told me all this?"

I drum my fingers on the table in front. This is the moment, the moment that could change everything between us.

I stall.

"Do you know what I found out in my twenties?"

"What?" She sets her nearly empty glass down before motioning to the server.

"The hair we donated at Tirupati…" I wait for her attention to return to me. It does. "That hair is sold in auctions. That hair is worth more than gold, even."

Her eyes get very round then. She sucks her lower lip and jerks her chin at me to proceed.

"They sell it to make wigs. Tirupati is one of the richest temples in the world. I wonder how much of that wealth results from the sale of our hair."

I sound bitter. I am bitter. All those devotees going in search of benediction, walking for miles, giving up their precious possessions, donating their hair — all feeding into a rapacious, materialistic, heartless machine.

"You know," her voice is soft now, faltering. "You know that I still believe."

I've seen the crucifix in her room. I know she does. Sometimes it reminds me of our kitchen shelf where all the various gods hung out together, having a laugh at our expense. Us poor gullible idiots.

"You're a good Christian girl."

She flicks me a nervous glance before looking away.

We both stare into the horizon together.

"What happened to them all? Your father? Your brothers? Your family?"

"Valiya Ammayi passed about ten years after Amma. Appa died four years ago. The boys have grown into men. Strange men who lord it over their wives and look at me like I'm some sort of circus freak."

"And your aunt? Baby?" She can't hide the smirk. I know. It's a silly name for a grown woman.

"Ah." I lean back into my chair. "Her."

"What?"

"She's still alive."

"And?"

"Totally loony, of course. She held it together for a while and then lost it completely. We had her committed to a mental asylum quite some years ago."

"Gosh!"

"Yeah."

"And you really think she placed a spell on your mother?"

Oh Daisy! I look at her blue eyes, her golden hair cascading in waves down her shoulders, her pink lips parted in question, and sigh.

"Yes, I really do believe that Baby Aunty wished Amma ill, and whether she really placed a spell on her is immaterial. The fact is that the moment she entered our home, she destroyed everything good in it."

"Divya," she places a hand on mine and a delicious shiver goes through me. "Can I give you an alternative version?"

I snatch my hand back, but she carries on regardless.

"Your mother was already sick, your aunt was grieving for a life she couldn't have, and you needed someone to blame."

"That's not true!" I feel my throat close up, tears of anger threatening to spill from my eyes.

That's when she leans forward and kisses me lightly on my lips.

"It's okay. You were a child, you didn't know any better."

I pull her towards me and crush her lips beneath mine. My fingers tangle in her hair, and as she responds to my touch, I feel the weight of my grief, of my long-held fury and resentment, fall away. I want to —I need to drown in her, in this sublime, glorious moment. I need this to soothe my bruised heart, my wretched soul.

Her fingers touch my hair.

"It's never easy to let go of the past. I'm going to try, but I need you to try, too." Her voice is soft, pleading.

I nod mutely.

"Divya?"

"Yes?"

"Grow your hair. Grow it back for me?"

Grow my hair? Let the thickness of it graze my cheeks and fall upon my shoulders? Lie in the sunshine and let my locks dry naturally?

A sweet jasmine perfume wafts through the air, and I think, yes.

Yes. I think I'm ready.

THE FAKE ROLEX

She loved him, of course. It didn't matter that he didn't love her back, that he *couldn't* love her back. Not in the way she wanted him to. None of that mattered.

He stood in front of the audience in his usual black turtleneck and black jeans. Supremely confident on the surface. Sexy, suave, bitingly funny; his dark wavy hair gelled back from his face, and his long-lashed grey eyes focussing on the people he wanted to impress—the ones who would have laughed no matter what tall tale he told. She wanted to tell him to stop. *Stop trying to impress them. They're already in your pocket.* But she understood why he did it. If it weren't for them, how would he survive?

Venice in autumn.

She wouldn't have chosen to be here, but here he was and she'd had no choice in the matter, really. The canals were worse in the summer. They stank of sewage, but a local had once told her it was just naturally occurring seaweed and mud. Anyway, it wasn't the smell that bothered her. It was the hordes of tourists—all pushing and shoving, jostling to get the best picture near the Rialto as they moved like swarms of insects, corrupting and polluting as they went along.

Autumn was better. She was glad that this party, this celebration of a silver wedding anniversary, was in October. So much quieter than the summer.

Gabriel finished his anecdote with a flourish. They clapped.

"Bravo!" the woman in the amethyst silk dress called out. She was nearly fifty but unashamed about undressing him with her eyes. So it was. So it always was.

He smiled back at the woman, murmuring something into her ear before moving off. His eyes searched for her, and she raised her hand from the back of the room. *Here I am. I'll never abandon you. I'll go wherever you go.*

He walked towards her, panther-like in his gait, and she observed him dispassionately once again. There was something deliberate about his handsomeness, as if he had cultivated it; grown it out of the seeds of his genes into something so much more captivating than it was originally meant to be. His lean body, his cheekbones enhanced with just the tiniest bit of fillers, those lush lips touched with the barest hint of rouge, the rich, musky cologne that cost a bomb, the shoes that were handmade from the finest Italian leather, the uniform of black that stood out in stark contrast against the paleness of his complexion — his was a Byronesque beauty. Arrogant and passionate; capable of destruction, of annihilation. She knew only too well.

Outside, the gondoliers called out, "*Òe!*" Shouts of greeting to one another.

In the early evening hour when the mutinous glow of the setting sun had created ripples of red gold on the water, as they had disembarked from their private gondola on to the steps of the Palazzo where the party was, the gondolier had looked into her eyes and said, "*Sei una bella ragazza.*"

Gabriel had laughed and said, "All Italian men are flirts. It is part of our nature."

Still, she held the compliment close to her heart, letting it warm the cold and hungry corners of it.

Now, as he strode towards her, she schooled her face into its usual adoration. Gabriel expected it of her, and how could she deny him?

"What did you think?"

"It was perfect."

"Was it enough?"

"I think so."

"Signora Oteri isn't here yet though, is she?"

"I haven't spotted her."

"She's the one, I hear. The one who is a hard nut to crack. She is so used to people fawning over her."

He looked worried for a moment, his forehead creasing. She reached forward and touched his brow.

"It will be okay. You'll see."

Her words had the desired effect, and he stopped frowning immediately, bestowing her with his magical 1000-watt smile. Her heart clenched. Even after all these years, his smile had the power to melt all her defences, wash away all her petty grudges and reduce her to the lovesick puppy she had once been.

"You." He said that one word before kissing her swiftly on the head, then moved away to mingle once again.

She patted down her hair and looked around. She knew no one here, and she was not a conversationalist. She preferred observing. Right now, though, she needed a break from that too.

She plucked a glass of Prosecco from the server's tray and headed outside towards the balcony. There was still a faint orange glow on the horizon, but night had descended over Venice, bringing its own bewitchment with it.

As the orange melded into the blue of the Adriatic Sea, the sun took one last sigh before sinking into slumber, and the waters gradually turned from vivid cerulean to glinting sapphire to an inky, impenetrable navy blue. Yet around her, the lights cast their own reflections upon the dark waters, like ladies shedding their cloaks before entering a ballroom. Beneath those shimmers lay the secrets of this floating city. La Serenissima, the Grande dame of Italy, a faded beauty of exquisite charm.

The air had the tiniest chill to it, and she drew her pashmina tightly around her. The wind carried the heavy and rich fragrances of the bedecked women in the ballroom, and the smoky and sweet aromas of the cigars that the bow-tied men smoked.

She closed her eyes and inhaled, allowing the city to whisper its secrets to her. It spoke of the slow and inevitable decay of the stone foundation beneath her, the silent encroachment of the waters upon the edifice of man's constructions, the multiple dreams and desires of its inhabitants. The loves that were, the loves that would be, and the loves that never could be.

She let the breeze caress her face as she leaned on the balustrade. The sound of clinking glasses and laughter receded for a bit as she let her mind wander the canals of her memories.

How indubitably the past was linked to the present. How intertwined every action was with its consequence. Which turn had led her here? Which decision had mapped out her destiny?

"Beautiful, no?" The gruff voice came from somewhere behind her, and she spun around so quickly that the Prosecco splashed out of her glass.

"*Signorina*," the shadow apologised. "I didn't mean to startle you."

The shadow moved closer, and she saw the man. Hair greying at the temples, tanned skin, sad eyes.

"I... I'm sorry," she said. "I was miles away."

"Where?"

"Pardon?"

"Where were you? How many miles?"

She smiled then, and he returned her smile, joining her at the balustrade.

"Mind if I smoke?"

She shrugged and took a sip of her Prosecco. He lit up a thin Cohiba cigarillo.

"Why is an attractive woman like you standing alone?"

She cast him a sidelong glance and turned towards the water again.

"For some peace and quiet." She hoped he would pick up the

reproach in her voice and leave, but he stayed there, blowing out the rich tobacco smoke into the wind.

"Then you are in the wrong city. Venice is glamour and decadence, luxury and extravagance. For peace and quiet, you must go elsewhere."

She wondered if he was laughing at her.

"I had hoped I could be alone with my thoughts for a while." Now she didn't care if she offended him.

"That is never a good idea." He moved closer to her, the wool of his sleeve brushing the bare skin of her arm. "Thoughts must pass through your mind like clouds in the sky. If they stay too long, they make thunderstorms."

Now she knew he was laughing at her. She pulled her pashmina closer and moved away slightly.

"Are you a guest here?" It was a silly question, but she had never been good at small talk.

"In a way." He gave her another enigmatic smile. "And you?"

"In a way, too."

"But we hide here, away from the festivities."

"I wasn't hiding. I was enjoying the sunset."

"Ah yes, our glorious sunsets must be enjoyed. But not in solitude."

"Alessandro!" a woman's voice called out, and the man turned towards it.

"I am here," he replied. "I will come in soon."

She looked at the silhouette of the woman. Statuesque. Beautiful, no doubt.

"Your wife?"

"My sister," he responded with a sigh. "Dinner is being served. We must go in."

"I will, in a moment."

"Then I shall leave you with your thoughts. Mind they do not create any rain, *signorina*."

As he walked away, she felt a certain sadness envelop her. She had wanted him to go, but now she wanted him to stay. She finished the last of her Prosecco, then dropped the glass into the dark waters below, watching it float for a moment before being swallowed into the depths.

⁂

The table was a hundred and twenty feet long and nearly eight feet wide. It was made entirely out of glass, with an antique gold frame supporting it. Each chair was upholstered in white-and-gold damask, the pattern mirroring the crystal chandeliers hanging above the table. People were already seating themselves, having consulted the large chart of place settings at the doorway to the dining room.

She looked for her name and then looked to see how far Gabriel was seated from her. He had forewarned her that much of this evening would be spent networking and that she would have to amuse herself. She didn't mind. Most of her life had been spent that way, anyway.

She found herself seated between two men. One was a stout man with a florid face who beamed at her as she sat down. The other was an elegant, slender man with a hook nose, who cast her an imperious glance and turned away. She knew which dinner companion she preferred, but smiled politely at the man on her right, willing him to turn away too.

He said something to her in Italian, and she shook her head, indicating that she didn't understand.

"*Inglese?*"

"*Si.*"

"'Ow are you here?" he asked in heavily accented English, but before she could formulate a reply, she felt movement next to her. When she turned, her terrace companion had replaced the elegant man on her left.

"You needed rescuing." He smiled at her, his eyes crinkling at the corners.

She smiled back, her relief evident. Had it been that obvious?

"I didn't, but thank you anyway."

He leaned across her and said something in rapid fire Italian to the man on her right, who puffed out his cheeks and turned away from her in a huff.

"Giorgio is insufferable," he said in an undertone. "You would have been trapped in Dante's Inferno for the next two hours."

He wiggled his eyebrows at her, and she laughed.

"I doubt that, and how do I know that you are any better?"

He grinned before saying, "You don't. But *bellissima*, you have two hours to find out."

At the very top of the table were two large, gilt-edged chairs for the host and hostess. As they arrived to take their places, a violinist started to play *'L'autunno'* from Vivaldi's Four Seasons.

"It's quite spectacular!" she gasped.

"What is? The music?" He looked amused.

"Everything."

There were white orchids in gold vases filling the room with their heady scent. Little flames danced on tapered Aurelian candles while tea lights set in gilt mesh holders basked under their glow. The damask patterned plates seemed too delicate to even touch, the heavy gold cutlery serving as a counterpoint to them. The lace edged napkins had a centuries old look about them, as if handed down from generation to generation.

"Signora Oteri has exquisite taste." She looked towards the hostess, who had just seated herself at the head of the table.

The lady was dressed in a long black silk dress with a plunging neckline. Nestling between the orbs of her magnificent breasts was a large, pear-shaped emerald surrounded by smaller diamonds. Her face was round and not unkind. She couldn't make out the colour of her eyes, but knew that they were the same green as the emerald. Gabriel had told her.

Next to her, the stooped and wizened old man, almost thirty years her senior, seemed to disappear into his chair. Signor Oteri belonged to one of the oldest families in Venezia. He came from money. Old money.

"Are you always this easily impressed?"

"Easily?" She looked at him. "I'm not sure which circles you move in, but not everyone dines in such fine surroundings."

Her mind flashed back to dinners in front of the television, a tray on her lap, trying to shut out the raised voices in the background.

"Tell me," he picked up her name card from the table and glanced at it, "Grace," he set it down again, "what brings you to these fine surroundings?"

"Work." She was short with him, annoyed by his presumption.

"What kind of work?"

But now a server was offering her wine, while another placed an appetiser of quail eggs *crostini* and grated *pecorino* in front of her.

Suddenly, she realised how ravenous she was; how she hadn't eaten all day, her stomach twisted in anxiety for this evening.

She ignored his question, tucking into the food with relish. Delicate and tiny as the portion was, it was still mouth-wateringly delicious. Italy had never disappointed when it came to food.

A moment later, she looked up to meet his dark eyes watching her. He hadn't touched his own appetiser.

"I don't know your name," she blurted out stupidly before realising that she did. The woman at the door had called him Alessandro.

His lips twitched again. Everything she said or did, he found amusing. She had never thought of herself as an oaf, but in his presence, she felt like one.

"I'm Alessandro Molena. It is a pleasure to meet you, Grace."

She set down her knife and fork and took his proffered hand. His clasp was warm, and suddenly, she didn't feel like an oaf anymore. She felt like a woman, a beautiful, desirable woman. She hadn't felt this way in years.

She withdrew her hand and fumbled with the napkin in her lap. In the distance, over the hubbub of many small and large conversations surrounding her, she heard Gabriel laugh. It was high-pitched and false, a contrivance that had started to irritate her.

When the main course of *Fegato alla Veneziana* arrived, she found she had lost her appetite.

"It is our specialty," Alessandro said. "The chef has used figs also with the onions."

"Oh," she said, looking down at her plate.

"You do not like it."

"No," she shook her head, "I just… I am not that hungry after all."

"Then drink the *Sangiovese*. It comes from Signor Oteri's own vineyard and it is simply sublime."

So she drank the wine, hoping she could just for this one moment enjoy the attention of an attractive man and forget all about Gabriel.

※

Some guests had already left by the time they moved into another room of the Palazzo. Just twenty of them remained in the room. The lights were dim, and people clustered around the host and hostess, seating themselves at vantage points. She took a chair in the corner, sipping on her limoncello quietly. Her eyes felt heavy now, the effect of too much wine and too little food.

Alessandro had disappeared after dinner, and she wondered if he had left. But Gabriel was here. He had ingratiated himself into Signora Oteri's orbit, and was whispering to her, their heads bent together. Signor Oteri sat next to her in a plush armchair, looking even more cadaverous up close.

Now the woman in the amethyst silk dress spoke up.

"Hello, everyone! *Un momento di attenzione, per favore*. Please to listen to me."

Her English was heavily accented, but most people seemed to understand her. The guests had come from various parts of the world —from Australia, Singapore, Dubai and America, and the many accents Grace had heard over the course of the evening had melded into an incomprehensible babble in her head. But this woman's English had an unmistakable charm and brought back memories of another time, other voices that had spoken haltingly, overlaid with the heaviness of another tongue.

"Gabriel here has been a discovery! A real jewel," the woman simpered into her drink. "I wanted him to come here, to meet all of you, especially Signora Oteri. You see, not only does he source the most beautiful jewels for us from Africa, he is also a source of much *divertimento*. His stories…"

She watched Gabriel watching the woman. She saw how his back straightened and his shoulders pulled back, how his tongue flicked out and licked his lips, how his entire body vibrated with a suppressed energy. He was ready. Oh yes, he was ready to take centre-stage. To impress these rich women and their indulgent husbands, and to source the blood diamonds they wore so proudly on their earlobes and wrists. Eager to take over from their fusty family jewellers, to undercut the more respected establishments, and make inroads into the very heart of Venetian *Alta società*. To conquer the world if he could. He was a hustler, and nothing gave him more joy than finding a new playground. The more rarefied the better.

"Come," the woman called out to him, and he almost tripped over his feet in his haste, but caught himself just in time, slowing down and proceeding with the elegance he prided himself on. This was his moment, and he would not squander it recklessly. Every eye was on him as he stood next to the curvy brunette.

"Sophia," he purred, "is much too kind. She is like the rare ruby that adorns her person. Beautiful, extravagant, and rich." He winked at her and she laughed delightedly in response. There was an echo of polite laughter from the audience, but he was only warming them up at this point.

"It's true that I collect rare and beautiful jewels from all over the world, but in my travels, I collect something else as well." He paused long enough for his gaze to travel over the well-heeled crowd before pausing just a beat longer on Grace. Then his gaze moved on and settled on Signora Oteri. "I collect stories."

He smoothed down the lapel of his dinner jacket, a reflexive action she knew well. He was about to launch into one of his many tales. She wondered which one, and then she wondered again where Alessandro had gotten to.

SIX - STRANGE STORIES OF LOVE

"Today I will tell you a story I have never told before. Something I witnessed firsthand and it could rival the best opera in the world."

Now he had them where he wanted them. Curious, excited, ready. Eager to lap up whatever outlandish yarn he was about to spin.

"This is a story of love. Of passion and anger. Of betrayal and revenge. It is also a true story."

Sophia retreated to a chair. Someone dimmed the lights even more so that only a faint glow remained and most people were in the shadows. Not Gabriel. He stood under the dimmed chandelier and the light it cast bathed him in honeyed gold. A server came around with more cigars for the men and liqueurs for the women. She shook her head in refusal, still nursing her drink. Tonight's indulgence would cost her dearly tomorrow. She was a lightweight with alcohol, something Gabriel found endlessly amusing.

"The woman was Italian. A Sicilian cousin, and you know how they are."

The laughter was more full-throated now.

"She was beautiful when she was young. So beautiful that boys would fall off their bicycles when riding past her. With this big *meloni*," he held out his hands in front of his chest indicating the size of the melons, "could you blame them?"

Everyone laughed at the crudeness of the gesture, so at odds with their sophisticated surroundings. He carried on, seemingly unaffected.

"She was so beautiful that even before she turned sixteen, she had twenty proposals for marriage. But she was a clever one. She didn't want to stay stuck in a little village, however charming, when her looks were her passport to escape her overbearing mother and her overprotective father."

He took a cigar from the server and lit it in a practised move.

"However, her beauty was like an overripe peach. Succulent, but on the verge of decay. Her mother warned her often, seeing her own looks disappear in her late twenties. She would tell her to marry a stable man like her father, build a home, have children, and be content. But Gina, shall we call her Gina? Oh, Gina was a flighty one.

She had no interest in turning into another Sicilian mama with an apron around her ample waist. She wanted to land herself a rich man. One who would wine and dine her, ply her with silks and jewels and take her on long cruises on the Mediterranean."

Signora Oteri's eyes gleamed with a secret fire, but she shrouded them with her lashes, her left hand stroking the silk of her dress while the right reached for Signor Oteri's hand.

"Gina held out long enough for one such man to come along. He was an Englishman, the second son of a Lord, no less."

Grace shivered. Someone had opened a door and let a draught in. A moment later, that someone was standing behind her. She knew without turning that it was Alessandro.

※

"Now, what our poor Gina didn't know was that this man, shall we call him Robert? This man was only living off the crumbs from his father's table. On his own, he was useless. A handsome but useless ornament."

Gabriel took a deep drag on his cigar, and everyone waited with bated breath for him to proceed. Alessandro noiselessly pulled up a chair next to her. She didn't turn to acknowledge him. Her eyes were on Gabriel, her skin turning to gooseflesh as she screamed internally, *no, no, no.*

"At first she had the lifestyle. They travelled first class everywhere, ate out in the best restaurants, and lived in the west wing of his father's enormous country pile. She thought she had it made."

"Then?" Signora Oteri's gaze was on him with a laser-sharp focus, her query breathless.

"Then," Gabriel smiled at her benignly, "*quando sei nella merda fino al collo.* The shit hit the fan."

Grace dug her nails into her palm.

"You see, although the old Lord had been quite fond of the Sicilian firecracker his son had married, with her flirtatious ways, her charmingly accented English, her curves that delighted his fading eyes, his older son had seen right through her grasping, money-grabbing ways. There was no love lost between the two, and even less between the sisters-in-law. One, a pure-bred racehorse from the Home Counties, and the other, a wild filly of indeterminate origin."

There was an audible gasp from his audience. They felt insulted, but that suited him fine as he grinned in a relaxed manner.

"Now, now. I'm only telling you what the English saw. We know what they're about too, don't we?"

Once again they relaxed, united in their dislike for the neighbours who had Brexited them as if they were a superior species, and every European a nuisance to be rid of their lands.

"This was when Gina started to realise that all that glitters isn't gold. Heavily pregnant with her first child, she saw her husband start and fail at many ventures until the only thing they had remaining was the small amount of interest from the sum his father had invested wisely for his useless son, in anticipation of this very outcome."

He ran his fingers through his hair and smiled once again at the onlookers.

"To her credit, Gina did not give up on The Honourable Robert straight away. She remained loving and supportive, hoping he would turn their fortunes around. But it was not to be. Robert had neither the business acumen of his late father, nor the connections that his brother had fostered over the years. Frankly, Robert was a bit of a waste of space, really."

Grace bit her lip and looked down. That's when Alessandro leaned in and whispered, "He's a bit of a *bastardo* himself, no?"

Grace shot him a quick glance before turning her attention back to Gabriel.

"They had to move into a two bed terraced house in a modest neighbourhood, and once Gina discovered that upward mobility had been snatched from her forever, she unleashed the furies on her husband. Robert grew quieter and more desperate, and she grew into a shrew."

Tired of standing, Gabriel pulled up a chair to sit in. As he sat down, everyone inched their chairs forward, too.

"There is a certain kind of woman," he continued, "who will never let a man live down his shortcomings. She will remind him as soon as he wakes up, she will harangue him all day long, and the last thing he will hear before he goes to bed is just how much of a failure he is. Gina was just that woman."

"Everyone in the neighbourhood would hear their quarrels. Neighbours started stepping in when things got a bit too 'boisterous', shall we say? There was a little girl in the household, a mousy little thing, who lived in the shadow of her mama's infamous rages and her father's careless ineptitude."

A tear trickled down Grace's cheek, and she wiped it away hastily before Alessandro spotted it.

"The kindly Italian lady two doors down all but adopted the little girl, giving her a haven, away from the daily dramas and diatribes of her volatile mother. As for Gina, as her mother had predicted, she became the blowsy beauty you admire from afar, but steer clear of as soon as you see her up close. Her anger and her frustration were spelt out all too clearly in the two vertical lines between her brows, in the way her mouth turned down at the corners, and in the way she neglected to take care of her house or her child."

"*Che triste*," Signora Oteri murmured.

"Sad, yes, but not the end of the tale." He sat back and took another deep drag of the cigar. "Meanwhile, the older brother had produced no offspring with his thoroughbred wife, and when he died unexpectedly in a Polo accident, guess who inherited the peerage?"

"Oh's" and "Aaahs" greeted this pronouncement.

"The worthless Robert had suddenly become a Lord, and Gina, the Lady of the Manor. A position she had coveted for a long, long time."

He looked around him, and suddenly his gaze was on her, and even though Grace was sitting in the shadows, she felt it penetrate her very core.

"This could have been a happy story, one with ups and downs, failures and successes, but one that ended well, nonetheless. That would be boring." He clicked his fingers. "And this is not that story."

"In preparation for her elevated role in society, Gina became all hoity-toity with her neighbours. Even the gentle Italian lady, Giuseppina, someone who had considered herself a friend and a confidante, was given short shrift. Her simple God-fearing husband, Luigi, who had put up with having another child underfoot, his wife's time taken up by another household's problems, was not spared either. Nor was their young son. Suddenly, they were beneath her. The very people who had taken care of her little girl, and had put up with Gina turning up at their door at all odd hours, were treated as if they were mud beneath her shoes. But as the proverb goes, *'la superbia andò a cavallo e tornò a piedi'*. Gina had counted her chickens much before they had hatched."

Grace pulled the pashmina around her tighter. She felt cold, both inside and out.

❧

Alessandro leaned towards her and whispered, "Would you like to leave?"

She shook her head.

"Then let me get you something to warm you." He discreetly called over a server . *"Puoi portare un espresso per la signorina?"*

She didn't want an espresso but couldn't trust herself to speak, so she stayed mute and accepted the care he was offering.

Of all the betrayals, this had to be the worst. Gabriel had sworn to her, *sworn* that this story would always remain between them. Yet here he was peddling it out for cheap laughs. He'd have a justification afterwards. He'd say, "But no one knows it's about you!" Or "I changed the names, didn't I?" Or even worse, "What does it matter after all these years? Whom do you owe your allegiance to, huh?"

Whom did she owe her allegiance to? The parents who had neglected her, abandoned her, forgotten her, or the boy who had rescued her?

Grace was fifteen when her uncle had died. A quiet, mousy girl who took after her father. She didn't have her mother's beauty or her temperament. And although she understood her frustration, she loved her father too much to care that they were not wealthy and titled. This had been the only life she had known, and while it wasn't exactly happy, it was enough. For her.

Then Papa inherited the title and the manor.

"That should have been the end of their problems," Gabriel carried on, "But it was only the beginning of new ones."

The server took away the spent cigar, and Gabriel stretched his legs out, crossing his arms in front of his chest.

"You see, these old country manors need money to upkeep. Robert had none. While Gina was already planning a lavish, and no doubt tasteless, renovation of the place, Robert was counting the pennies. His brother had left all his stocks, bonds, and investments to his wife. Shall we call her Lady Rose? As was her right, of course. Robert knew that he would have to come to some sort of agreement with his estranged sister-in-law."

Those days were a blur in her mind. It had come as a shock to her that they would be moving away, leaving Mama Giuseppina, Papa Luigi, and her beloved Gabriel behind. They were more than family to her. They were everything.

"So Robert told Gina to be patient. He said it would be a while before they moved, that she had waited years and a few more months were nothing in comparison. Gina didn't take it well. Here she had been lording it over everyone in the neighbourhood, and suddenly she was stuck here for longer? Eating humble pie was not her style. So, she stomped her feet and threw one hissy fit after another, but, for once, Robert stood firm."

Cold autumn mornings, her mother screaming at her father downstairs while Grace burrowed deeper into bed, pulling the covers over her head. Cold autumn mornings that would lead to a bleak, bleak winter.

"How long is this man's story?" Alessandro sighed. "It isn't even that interesting."

Grace swallowed a sob. No, it wasn't interesting. It was devastating.

"Weeks turned into a month, and then two. Gina's birthday was a fortnight before Christmas and she demanded that Robert buy her something expensive for all the patience she had exhibited."

"On the morning of her birthday, she unwrapped a large box to reveal a gold Rolex watch. For once, Gina was speechless. She had wanted a Rolex watch for years. In the early days of their marriage, Robert had promised her one, and then failed to deliver. Just as he had failed to deliver on so many other promises. But suddenly, there it was, this marvel of a watch. The apex of watch manufacturing—beautiful, discreet, reliable, consistent. None of that mattered to Gina. For her, it was a status symbol. It meant that at long last, she had arrived."

Gabriel paused for a moment. Then he asked for a glass of water.

For once in her life, Grace had seen another side to her mother, a happier, more content side. This was the woman her father had fallen in love with. No lines of discontent marred her face. She was happy, and that happiness radiated like the warm glow of a fireplace, heating her love-starved family.

"But," Gabriel set the emptied glass back on the server's tray before continuing, "what good is an expensive gift if you can't show it off? Gina had alienated herself from almost everyone in the neighbourhood by now. The only people who were willing to forgive her, to entertain her, were her Italian neighbours from two doors down. So, off she trotted a few days before Christmas, ostensibly taking them homemade cannoli, but really to dangle her wrist in front of her less well-off neighbours."

Grace remembered the day well. She had gone along with Mama, happy to bask in the glow of her elation, excited to see Gabriel, and content that Mama hadn't severed ties with Mama Giuseppina.

"She strutted in like a peacock asking to be admired, flaunting her gift, rubbing their noses in it. And they sat quietly, giving her everything she required once again."

He looked sad now. Maybe he was regretting telling the story. Or maybe he was regretting the part he had played. A sixteen-year-old boy whose anger fractured Grace's house.

. . .

"Luigi was a plumber by profession, but he had a secret hobby. One that was secret from everyone except his wife and son. He loved watches. Tinkering with them, fixing them, or collecting them when he could afford one. Over the years, he had collected a fair few, hoping they would come in handy for his son. A little nest egg of sorts to start him off in life."

"It had begun when Luigi had inherited an old Omega Seamaster from his father, who had told no one in his family how he came by the watch. But it had been his prized possession and then, after his death, it became his son's."

Gabriel pulled down the sleeve of his shirt. Grace knew that he didn't want anyone spotting the Omega on his own wrist, the only watch he'd held on to after all this time, the rest sold to raise capital for his business. The sick feeling in the pit of her stomach had settled. All she felt now was dread, and the recognition that her life had become some kind of joke to these people. Alone and alienated, she had been let down once again by someone she loved.

"When Gina flaunted her watch in front of them, he immediately picked up on the fact that the watch was a fake. A good one, but a fake nonetheless. He stayed silent, allowing the woman to gloat, knowing that a man who could gift his wife a fake watch had very little regard for her. He felt sorry for her and stayed silent. Yet, at night, when Giuseppina discussed their neighbour's good fortune, Luigi gently told her the truth, hoping that his words would reveal to her that his love for her was unwavering and incapable of deceit."

Everyone had fallen silent, waiting to hear what happened next. Grace wanted to stand up and scream. *How dare you mock my family? How dare you!* But she didn't dare, because if it hadn't been for Giuseppina and Luigi, where would she have gone? Who would have taken her in? They had been more of a family to her than her own.

"What neither Luigi nor Giuseppina knew was that their son had overheard their conversation, and filed it away to use at a future date. This boy loathed Gina. He loathed the way she treated her husband and child, the way she conducted herself around the people in her

SIX - STRANGE STORIES OF LOVE

community, but most of all, how she treated his good and kind parents who had shown her nothing but care and compassion."

Gabriel cleared his throat, and the server brought him another glass of water almost immediately. He took it and flashed him a smile of thanks. Then he took a sip and set the water down by the side of his chair.

"Meanwhile, Gina was on her best behaviour, reassured by the expensive gift, content that soon she would be ensconced in her manor and could leave all the trappings of her lean days behind her. Imagine her surprise then when Robert declared that they would have to sell their terraced home to fund the move! Gina had never been one for facts and figures. All she knew was that suddenly the place she had called home for nearly sixteen years was to be sold. Still, if it was for a higher purpose, then she was willing to go along with it."

"Soon the FOR SALE board was up outside the house, and Gina started packing up their lives into multiple cardboard boxes in anticipation of the move. People traipsed in and out of the house, viewing it as a future home. Gina was at her genial best, reminding them that her own fortunes had changed under this very roof, and who was to say that theirs wouldn't?"

Grace remembered those days with a detached horror. Having to stay silent and polite as strangers walked into her room, commented on the posters on her wall, peeked out of her window onto the street below, opened her wardrobe doors and tutted at the mess inside. It had felt like an invasion. It had been an invasion.

"It was on one of those days, when they had almost closed the sale, that Gina came by again to see Giuseppina. This time, she had brought all the junk she needed to be rid of. Useless ornaments, faded curtains, a rug with a wine spill. Had there been even a single item of value—even sentimental value—then things wouldn't have blown up the way they did. But all of it was rubbish. Something that even a charity shop wouldn't accept. Yet there she was, trying to palm it off to her neighbours under the guise of doing good."

Gabriel paused his narrative, and from the way he clenched his hands, Grace knew that even today that single moment from the past had the power to reduce him to mute fury. She had glimpsed the hatred in his eyes that day and been shocked by it. But what she hadn't known was that his anger would no longer stay buried.

"The son left the room, unable to witness his mother's embarrassment or Gina's fake largesse. When he returned, he was holding an old Rolex in his hand. One from his father's slim collection. Gina saw him holding it and asked, "What is that you have there?" He smiled coldly and said, "It's my father's watch. And it's real, unlike the fake one you have on your wrist." Giuseppina gasped. She'd had no idea that her son knew. Gina simply laughed and left soon after. But the damage had been done. The seeds of doubt had been sowed."

Gabriel picked up the glass and took another sip. There were murmurs all around him. Alessandro leaned towards her and whispered, "I am so bored."

Grace sat stock-still, images from that day flashing in her mind. Mama dragging her to the local jewellers, her face turning to concrete when they told her the truth. Mama leaving her at home, calling for a taxi to go hunting for the man who had sold her a lie. The *pezzi i medda* she had married.

"Once Gina had confirmed that the boy had told her the truth, she went on the offensive. Her first job was to find Robert and find out what the hell he was up to."

Grace leaned forward now, despite herself. Like everyone else, she was on tenterhooks. Only, unlike everyone else, she knew how this story ended.

"If us Italiani are known for our passion, then the Siciliani, well, add a whole load of spice to that passion…"

Gabriel laughed, and everyone else laughed alongside. He was setting them up, easing them towards the cliff edge. Grace felt her hands go clammy.

"Robert was in so much trouble, he had no idea! I mean, the poor man, how was he to know? Gina had been too stupid to figure it out on her own, after all. But like a bloodhound with a scent in its nose, now that she knew, she wouldn't let go of the trail. And guess where the trail led her?"

"*Dove?*" Signora Oteri asked, her mouth open in an O. Then she corrected herself, and asked again, this time in English, "Where?"

"Straight to the bedroom of her former sister-in-law, Lady Rose, no less. She found them *in flagrante delicto!*"

Grace dropped her head. It was too much. She couldn't stay any longer. She scraped her chair back and ran outside. Someone called out to her, but she didn't hear. Blinded by the tears in her eyes, she grabbed at the handle of the nearest door and found herself on a terrace again. A different terrace, a different view, but away from it all —the memories, the pain, the sheer senselessness of it. She grabbed lungfuls of air, letting the tears stream down her face now. It was no good trying to hide it. It would always be there, like a gaping wound that would bleed through any number of bandages.

"You knew these people?" Alessandro asked from behind her, concern weaving itself through his words.

She nodded, still incapable of speech.

"Friends?"

"Parents," she said finally. Then the silence stretched between them interminably. When she couldn't bear it any longer, she turned to face him. His eyes were on the gently lapping water, his face devoid of expression.

"To laugh at someone's tragedy…"

"It's only a story to them."

"Yes."

They stood together and gazed upon the distant lights of San Marco.

"Perhaps that is the only way to get through sadness," he said, "to laugh at it."

She said nothing, allowing this quiet companionship to soothe her momentarily. When she spoke, it was almost reflective, as if all of it had happened to someone else.

"I am not a Lady, you know."

He turned towards her but remained silent.

"There was no title to inherit... after..."

He placed his hand on hers, and she felt the roughness of his palm against her soft skin.

"She died in prison, my Mama. Of pneumonia. She claimed right till the end that she hadn't meant to kill him, only frighten him. But the knife was sharp, and it severed through his carotid artery..."

"Shhh. Say no more." He took her in his arms then, and she rested her head upon his chest. It felt good, and in that moment she allowed herself to believe that if she wanted, really, really wanted, she could be free of the past.

Then the moment passed. The doors opened and more guests spilled onto the terrace, and she stepped away from him.

Signora Oteri made her way towards them, stopping short of Alessandro.

"So, this is where you have been hiding? And who is this lovely child?"

This was a woman in her prime, beautiful, confident, and loved. This could have been Mama, if her dreams hadn't turned to dust.

"Grace. Meet my sister, Beatrice."

She shook her hand politely, unsure of how much of a mess she looked, and how much could be seen in the dimness of the terrace.

"Grace. What a lovely name! You are here with Gabriel?"

"Yes," Grace whispered.

"Then you are a lucky woman indeed. He is *affascinante!*"

"I... I must freshen up." She fled in the direction of the toilet, avoiding looking at Alessandro.

The only accessible toilet was already occupied, so she turned the corner towards the one near the dining room.

Two figures hastily separated in a shadowy corner of the room. One of them was distinct in his carriage, the other one she recognised vaguely.

"Gabriel?" It came out in a strangled whisper. He emerged from the shadows, his hair mussed, shirt untucked. She didn't need to see any more. She ran into the toilet and locked the door behind her.

The retching started almost immediately. Memories engulfed her, attacking her like sharp little knives from all sides, until doubled up in pain, she sank to her knees.

"Grace?" It was Gabriel knocking. "Open the door!"

She wouldn't. She would stay here forever, hiding from everything out there.

"Please." She heard the supplication in his voice, the beginnings of an apology.

Dragging herself up, she opened the door. He came in and shut it behind him.

"Grace…"

She shook her head. She didn't want to hear it. Whatever it was, it could wait till tomorrow.

"Please," she asked, "can we go now? I'm exhausted."

"Yes, of course." He was solicitous now, and as he led her out, she felt another pair of eyes boring into her back.

※

Alessandro's persistence wore her down. Three days later, she agreed to meet him for a coffee. Gabriel was at work, so there were no excuses to be made.

Venice mid-morning was shimmering in the pale yellow sunlight, rising from her slumber like a lady of leisure. Even the waters lapped on the shores with a languid grace. There was something magical about this floating city, the city they predicted would be submerged in a hundred years. Everything had to die. Everyone, even.

He was already seated when she arrived, and he stood up as soon as he saw her. In the morning light, he looked older. His hair was more salt than pepper, and the grooves by the sides of his mouth, deeper. She estimated he was older than Signora Oteri by a couple of years, at least.

He pulled her chair out for her, taking her coat and hanging it on the peg behind them. She was glad he hadn't chosen a flashy place. The café was easy to overlook if one didn't know where to go. She had followed his instructions carefully, and now she was here, seated by a nook that faced the canal, as the sun rose high into the sky in the distance.

"I am glad you came," he broke the silence, his espresso sitting untouched in front of him. "What would you like?" He handed her the menu, but she merely shook her head. He didn't insist, but didn't let go of the menu, either.

"I..." she spoke softly, "I owe you an apology."

"No."

"Yes, yes, I do." She looked into his eyes, those blue eyes that looked pensive as they gazed upon her. "I misled you. That night... I led you to believe that I was single."

"You never lied."

"It was a lie of omission." She looked away. "If I gave you some sort of hope..."

"Hope, my lovely Grace, is not given. It lives in here." He touched his chest lightly as he met her eyes. "Why are you with him?"

"I love him," she answered.

"But he..."

"Doesn't love me. I know."

"I mean, a man such as him."

"I owe him everything."

"So it is gratitude that keeps you bound?"

"No," she shook her head again. "It's not as simple as that. I *know* him. I've looked into his soul, I have seen it bared, and despite everything—his anger, his flaws, his lies—I have *chosen* to love him."

Alessandro reached for his coffee and took a sip.

"Love is a complicated emotion."

"Yes." They were both quiet now, and she felt it again. This pull, this strange attraction to a man she had met only a few nights ago. A man full of secrets, too. Full of a sadness she wished to understand, but could not bring herself to ask.

"You married him," he said finally, as if trying to puzzle her out.

"It pleased Giuseppina. I was like a daughter to her. She wanted it so much for Gabriel, and also for me."

"Did she not see...?"

"Luigi knew. He told me not to, but I was too much in love to care."
"What kind of a life is it, to… to…"
"Not easy. But I knew what I was signing up for."
"And do you turn a blind eye when he?"
"Yes, I do."
Suddenly, he reached forward and took her hand.
"Why are you denying yourself happiness? He denies himself nothing! I've asked around and I know. He is a… a… *louche*!"
She withdrew her hand from his clasp.
"Alessandro, I have seen what lies and deception can do first hand. That is not the life I wanted for myself."
"That is the very life you are leading, *caro*! It is not he who is lying, it is you. All these years, you have misled yourself and believed that your heart was safe as long as you gave it to someone who cared very little for it. But in truth, this deception is eroding your soul. Is this what you really want?"
"I saw him, you know," she smiled through her tears. "That night. He was with that young boy, the server. I saw him. When he came towards me, there was nothing on his face. No contrition, no guilt. But why should there have been? He never hid his truth from me. It was I who was willing to take him on whatever terms he offered."
"It is still not too late. Here…" Alessandro scribbled something on a napkin and handed it to her. "Take my number. Anytime you need me, I'll be there. Just take it."
She took it, then stood up.
"Thank you, Alessandro."
He stood up and kissed her gently on her cheeks before handing her the coat from the peg. His musky cologne lingered on her lapel much after she had left him. She wandered the streets, unwilling to go back to the apartment just yet.
At noon, all shadows had shortened to nothing. Venice was silent and watching, her waters still, the reflections of her magnificent structures like paintings upon their glassy surfaces. She walked slowly, her steps faltering. Then she stood by and watched an older couple as they stood on a small footbridge, holding up a phone,

smiling into it as they clicked a selfie. They leaned into each other, their bodies conjoined. She watched every movement of theirs, waiting for them to finish before taking the steps herself. They smiled at her before moving off, holding hands as they went. Her heart felt hollow, leached of every emotion. Numb.

She stopped near another narrow bridge and gazed into the water. Her reflection stared back—still, austere, remote. Brittle like the branch she had snapped underfoot only moments earlier.

Grace took the napkin out of her pocket and looked at the digits Alessandro had scrawled on it. She stared at them as if trying to decipher a code. She crumpled it, then shook her head and smoothed it out before crumpling it again. Leaning on the balustrade, she held the napkin over the water, watching as a slight breeze ruffled its edges.

In the cloudless sky, the sun looked down on her in silence. Venice held her breath and her waters waited.

Grace stood there for a long time, arm outstretched, waiting for a sign. Then, with the tiniest shrug, she put the napkin back in her pocket and strode home.

KAROLINA

I think what struck me first was the all-cream outfit she was wearing. A cream polo neck with cream trousers, possibly silk. Cream shoes with pointed heels that had gotten stuck in a grating somewhere and torn midway up the heel. A suede jacket, and a handbag so tiny that not even a phone would fit in it. Cream too. She looked like the women from those billboards advertising some high-end boutique. Who wore cream and walked through the side alleys of Eighth Avenue? Cream outfits were for limousines and chauffeur-driven cars, not for walking around dirty old Manhattan.

She wasn't beautiful. No, I wouldn't have called her that. Her jaw was too square, her nose too hooked and her lips far too thin, even though she had lined them above their natural shape and filled them in with a soft gloss. Apricot blonde hair tied back in a chignon, pale blue eyes with thick mascaraed lashes, high cheekbones that belonged on a model except that she was fuller-figured than one, all curves, emphasized by the materials that skimmed and clung to her in the right places. She wasn't beautiful, but she was striking. You couldn't walk past her without turning to look once, maybe even twice.

Yet, women like her rarely stopped to have a chat with men like Jonas. Nor did they ask for a light, then stand under the awning of a

Thai restaurant to smoke a cheap cigarette, blowing smoke rings into the air, laughing throatily at a comment he'd made.

I sidled up to them, too awe-struck to say anything beyond a quick "hey" to Jonas.

"You ok, man?" he asked, turning his red-rimmed eyes to me. I nodded, looking between him and her, waiting for an introduction.

"This here is…" he paused, then looked at her.

"Karolina," she said, squinting into the distance, blowing another smoke-ring and watching it dissolve into the chilly evening air.

Sirens sounded two blocks away, waves of people rushed out from and towards Penn Station. A crew of flight attendants stood huddled under the awning of the hotel, waiting for their bus, while a businessman talked rapidly on his headset, shoving a slice of pizza into his mouth and cursing as the sauce spilled on his shirt. A baby bawled in the pram while his young mother yanked her toddler's hand, shouting at him in Spanish. Two hot chicas walked past, ready for their dates, their skirts barely covering the junk in their trunks. Friday evening in Manhattan.

"And you are?" She looked at me, her blue eyes impenetrable.

"Marty."

"Pleased to meet you, Marty."

She held out her hand, and I looked at it. Long fingers, perfectly manicured nails, soft clasp. My hand looked large and grimy, the dirt under my nails standing out in stark contrast against the cleanliness of her white skin. I withdrew my hand, hiding it in my pocket.

Later, much after she'd left, I asked Jonas what she'd wanted with him.

"Dunno, man. She comes around sometimes and has a chat. She bought me a burger once."

"Why does she want to hang out with bums?"

"Hey! Who you callin' a bum?"

"Us, man. That's what we are."

The bums of New York. Veterans of a long-forgotten war cast out onto the streets. No homes, no families, no healthcare. All we had was each other, our cardboard boxes and the good Lord, who rarely listened to our prayers.

The likes of Karolina didn't mingle with the likes of us. We were the dregs of humanity, washed up, forgotten, and largely ignored.

I'd belonged once, long ago. Had a family that cared, a mother who cried when I enlisted. Where were they now? The war had taken so much from me.

"You a better bum than me, Marty. You read books. You should talk to her. She's smart, like you."

Smart.

I'd been told that since I was a kid.

This here boy, Miss Martinez, is too smart for his own good.

Hey Smart Ass! Get outta my way.

Who you questionin', soldier? Think you're smarter than me?

Smart had got me nothing. Nothing but a shitload of trouble.

But it's true that I loved reading. Always had. My guilty pleasure was the collection of Harry Potter books that I had gathered over the years, carrying them in my knapsack from place to place, unwilling to part with even the ones that had pages missing. The story of a boy wizard who overcame his nemesis was an escape for a grizzled old veteran who was still fighting his demons from ten years ago.

I shook my head at Jonas before walking away. Tonight, it was about finding another place to sleep after the cops had cleared us out from the woods behind the Bronx Zoo.

"Where's Chris?" Jonas called out after me.

"Riding the subway," I called back. He'd ride it all night, just to have a warm place to sleep in. He'd ride it dead drunk, and sometimes I wondered if we'd find him dead on it too.

Seven more months.

Seven more months until I qualified for Safe Haven apartments. Seven more months until I'd have spent an entire year on the streets and been given 'street homeless' status. Seven more months of sleeping on park benches, hiding out in ATM lobbies, and hunkering down on church steps. What's seven months compared to ten years? I could do this.

It had taken me years to discover that alcohol wasn't my friend. Drowning out the memories didn't chase them away. They resurfaced repeatedly, pointing their fingers at me, saying, "You, you, you!"

When we were boys, we had fought with wooden sticks, pretending they were swords. We had lobbed balls at each other, play-acting as soldiers throwing grenades. We had held toy guns and shot invisible enemies.

Then we went to war, and the enemies were both visible and invisible.

I carry them with me now. All those people that I killed, and the ones that tried to kill me too. I should have died. So many of my friends had. Why was I spared? To wander the streets? To read Harry Potter? To exist because the alternative frightened me too much?

※

The next time I saw her, she was in a sky-blue sweater and ripped designer jeans, with canvas shoes that had blue rhinestones on them. She was sitting on the steps of the New York Public Library, her hands gesticulating wildly. Jonas was nowhere near, and I figured she was on the phone and had one of those ear pieces in. But as I got closer, I saw she was talking to herself.

"Hey, Karolina!" I mustered up the courage to greet her.

She looked at me and paused, then carried on talking.

"It's on the left. I said left. Yes, left. On the left."

I sat next to her on the steps, waiting for her strange monologue to end. People walking past gave us funny looks. I tried seeing us from their eyes. Here was an attractive blonde, clearly wealthy, sitting next to a man who slept rough, smelt funny and carried a knapsack that had seen better days. Still, it was New York, and people just walked on by.

It was another ten minutes of insisting that something was on the left before she stopped and looked at me properly.

"You're him," she said, tonelessly.

"I'm him," I agreed, not sure who the 'him' was.

"The one who likes Harry Potter." Her eyes were focussed on me with a strange intensity.

"Yes."

"My stepson liked those books, too. He read them all, over and over again."

"Yes."

"When his father sent him away, he thought he was going to a boarding school like the one in the book. Pig... pig..."

"Hogwarts."

"That one!" She sighed and leaned back, her elbows resting on the step behind her. "He's never forgiven us."

"How old is he?"

"Twenty-two now."

"I see."

"How old are you?" Her lips pursed as she looked me over.

"Fifty-five."

"Why do you read children's books?"

"They are not exactly..." I rubbed my hand over my beard. "I like them."

"Hmm."

We both stared ahead, watching people pound the pavement.

"Do you have a cigarette?" she asked.

"I don't smoke."

"Huh."

Mid-morning the traffic had eased slightly, and the sun was still gentle in the sky. A yellow cab spilled its contents onto the pavement in front of us—a family of Scandinavian tourists who spoke to one another in rapid Norwegian.

We watched them make their way to the lions flanking the museum, posing next to them, clicking photographs before going up the steps.

"I'm Austrian, you know," she said, watching them intently.

"You look it."

She laughed suddenly, her eyes crinkling, her lips opening up to reveal a set of dazzling white teeth. Too white. American white.

"We left when I was five. I'm not really Austrian. No more than you are Mexican."

I laughed alongside. That was a fair enough observation.

"So, Karolina?"

"Yes?" She was friendlier now. The ice between us had thawed.

"Why do you sit around with hobos?"

She stiffened and turned away. I thought I'd lost her then, that she wouldn't dignify my question with an answer. But she surprised me a few moments later.

"I have no other friends."

Jonas told me how he'd met her the first time. He'd been sitting outside Macy's during their annual flower show. Their windows had vibrant displays of spring blooms, attracting visitors from all over the world and the city. They weaved in and out of the store to admire and photograph the colorful blossoms. Jonas had parked himself near one entrance, hoping that his cardboard sign reading "Hungry and Homeless. Help!" would work its usual magic at this time of the year. It did. He made over fifty bucks on the first day. Then, on the fourth day, he felt someone drop next to him. It was her, and she was grinning at him as though they were old friends.

"I tell ya, man, it was weird," Jonas recalled as he puffed on his cigarette. "There she was, all fur coat and diamonds, sitting next to me. I thought I was goin' mad!"

"What did she want?"

"A smoke. She gave me ten dollars for it."

"What?"

"Yeah. I thought she was one of those do-gooders tryin' to get me into a shelter."

"What did you talk about?"

"Shoes." He poked his toe out of the large boot he was wearing.

"Shoes?"

"Yeah. She said you could tell a lot about a person by their shoes." He took another puff. "I mean, she made me laugh with some things she said... the way she spoke about all those people walkin' about."

"Did you become friends with her, then?"

"No way, man! She was bad for business. I had to tell her not to come back. I barely made twenty that day, and that's including the ten bucks she'd given me."

"Then, how?"

"A few months later, she saw me near Central Park and stopped for a chat. That's how we became friends."

"Does she still give you money?"

"Sometimes. But it ain't about that." Jonas glared at me. "She's lonely, Marty. She has no friends."

"How is that possible?"

Jonas stubbed out his cigarette on the grass and stood up.

"You haven't figured it out yet?"

I looked up at him and shook my head. Maybe I had, but I wanted him to say it. I needed to hear it.

"She ain't all there, man. Her head ain't right. If she wasn't rich, she'd be one of us."

🕮

They set Chris on fire when he was passed out. Kids on the subway. Probably thought it was funny. What's another drunk hobo to them, anyway? He'd fought for their country, and they set him on fire.

"Burnt to death, man." Jonas shook his head, then looked at his cigarette. His hands were shaking so badly he could barely bring it up to his mouth.

I didn't bother asking why. What was the point? We all had to die one day. If it wasn't a landmine that took him in the war, it would've been something else. He was barely alive as it was. Kids, though. I closed my eyes for a second. Chris had been a gentle giant, a man so incapable of hurting anyone that he had cried the first time he fired a gun. What a way to go. I made the sign of the cross and prayed he hadn't suffered too much.

"How many more months, Marty?" Jonas asked me, his eyes puffy and red.

"Five."

"You gotta get through the winter first."

"Yeah."

Winters were the worst. Even with all our clothes layered upon us, the cold would seep in. Ari had lost three fingers to frostbite last year. Jonas had lived under the scaffolding of a building in Boerum Hill.

"What about you, Jonas? They finished that building early this year. Where are you gonna go?" I asked, because I wasn't sure Jonas would get through another winter in the city. His lungs were weak, and that cough didn't sound too good either. "What about a shelter?"

Jonas shuddered.

"I didn't do a tour in Iraq to get stabbed in a shelter! They stole my shoes last time. I had to walk miles in my socks. Ain't goin' back there again!"

I nodded in understanding. I, too, would rather have faced the giant rats in Central Park than go to a shelter. But winter was a tough gig. We'd lost Ella to a fentanyl overdose. Sophie was beaten to death with a metal pipe, and Eric got pushed under a train by a schizo. New York could be worse than Iraq, in some ways.

"You could ask Karolina for her fur coat," I laughed.

"Nah, man. Ain't seen her in weeks." Jonas shrugged. He didn't get attached to people anymore. Not after his daughter had turned him out onto the streets.

"Where's she at? Haven't seen her around lately."

"Dunno. Last time she said something 'bout her ol' man givin' her a hard time."

"She got family?"

Jonas raised his eyebrows at me.

"Why you askin'?"

"Just."

"Now, you don't get lovesick for no rich white lady, Marty. Won't do you no good."

"Yeah."

❧

Jen had been my fiancée before they had sent me on my first tour. We had been looking at houses in Detroit, planning our babies and our lives together. We were childhood sweethearts who had met in church. Our families knew each other; our mothers bonded over their shared love of telenovelas. Jen didn't enjoy reading, but she watched the Harry Potter movies with me. We talked late into the night about Dumbledore and Voldemort; about good and evil, Heaven and Hell.

She couldn't handle the man I became. The one who came back from Iraq, who thrashed about in bed, screamed through his nightmares and woke up wild-eyed and soaked in sweat. It was too much Hell for her.

After the second tour, I didn't go home. Mami was dead, Papi had never been around, and Juan, my little sister's husband and I never saw eye to eye. There was no home to go to.

I came to New York instead.

Try as I did, hardly anyone would hire me. If they did, I got thrown out soon enough owing to turning up late and hungover, or not turning up at all. Cheap vodka got me through those years. Those years when I was just a drink away from oblivion, a needle away from an even worse fate.

But then I saw what it did to Ella.

She had been a model once. That's what she told us, anyway. Jonas scoffed behind her back. But I believed her. Behind the matted hair and the dead eyes, the skeletal frame and the yellowed teeth, I glimpsed a different Ella. One who strode catwalks and smiled at cameras. But they told her to lose weight, to become even thinner than she was. So she turned to heroin. And that was that.

❧

Book four was my favorite. It was the one in which they chose a champion for the Triwizard tournament. It was a thick old book, and so many pages were missing that anyone who hadn't read the book wouldn't have a clue as to what was going on. But I did. I had read it so many times over, I could close my eyes and recite whole passages. It gave me comfort, it did. This book and all the others painted a picture of a world where good could and would overcome evil. I wanted to believe that somewhere, such a world existed. That somewhere, all the senseless killing, the wars, the incendiary devices that blew people to smithereens, served a higher purpose.

Mami had always said that God had a plan for all of us. I wish I knew what His plan for me was. I know He had saved me from alcoholism by sending Father Escamilla to me when I was on the brink of death. Father Escamilla had taken me in and dried me out. He had tried to turn me into a different man, but the lure of the streets was too much. By then, I had been a nomad too long to want to settle in one place. The irony was that ten years down the line, I was desperate for that one place to settle down in. But Father Escamilla was dead, and there was no one to vouch for me anymore. Five more months of living on the streets before I could get a roof over my head.

I could do it.

"I've taken my medication today," she said, laughing, sitting between Jonas and me.

In a shocking pink sweater and gray jeans, she looked a lot younger than her forty-plus years. Younger and fresher. Her cheeks were flushed and her eyes looked bright. She looked like a woman who had just taken a jog or been making love all morning. I had a sudden urge to reach forward and kiss her.

"I got a book for you, Marty." She reached into her large pink bag that had CELINE stenciled on it. "Look."

I looked. It was 'The Complete Works of Shakespeare.'

"Thought it was time you moved on from those children's books." She grinned at me.

"They're not..." I sighed and took the large leather-bound book out of her hands. "Thank you."

"Don't thank me. It's my husband's copy. I stole it this morning from the library. Serves the asshole right!"

"How's your ol' man?" Jonas asked, giving the book a suspicious look, as if it were bugged or something.

"Oh, he's having an affair." She waved her hands lightly. "I found out a week ago."

"Damn, woman! What you gonna do?"

She bit her lip and looked down at her shoes. Suddenly, all the cheeriness she had been filled with vanished.

"I don't know, Jonas. I've been married to him for twenty years. I can't just walk away now. There have always been other women, I've known that. But this time, it's different."

She took a deep breath.

"He's not hiding it this time. He wants me to know."

"Why?" I was confused by the situation, by her.

"I think he wants to leave me, but he'd prefer it if I left him."

"Why don't you?"

She laughed. "And do what? Go where?"

Just then a garbage truck trundled by, the stench of rotting waste filling our nostrils.

"I am like garbage. Nobody wants me." She looked sad as she plucked at a fiber on her sweater.

"Have a cigarette, Karolina." Marty offered her the last one in his pack, and she accepted it graciously.

We sat together, watching as the late afternoon pedestrians walked by us and threw curious looks our way. One even threw a dollar at Jonas' feet.

"I could join you," she said brightly. "We could be like the Musketeers. One for all, all for one."

"Dunno who they are," Jonas grumbled, "and they better not be comin' round here. This here is our patch."

"Karolina," I looked at her, "this life isn't for you. It's not what you think it is. We are bums. No one wants us, and if anything happened to one of us, no one would miss us neither."

"That's just like me then," she declared, smiling broadly and linking arms with us.

Another time. The air had started getting chillier and winter wasn't too far off.

"Do you believe in Karma?" Her hair was all over the place, and the black sweater she wore was frayed at the sleeves. Today was not a good day for her, but at least she was lucid.

"Karma?" Jonas asked, "Who's that?"

"It's not a who," I explained. "It's a belief that if you do bad stuff, it comes back to you."

"So, what did I do, huh? And you? We just followed orders." Jonas stomped off, kicking the lid of a garbage can to one side.

"So?" she asked me again, her voice low, her eyes full of unshed tears.

"I believe in God," I answered after a beat, not sure what she wanted from me.

"I believed a long time ago, too." The tears fell now, down her cheeks, onto the clasped hands in her lap.

"What happened, Karolina?"

She stayed silent, and I waited. Then she spoke in a rush of words, as if she couldn't wait to get them all out; to spill everything like the tears that streamed steadily out of her lowered eyes.

"They never wanted me. My sister was already eleven when I appeared. I was an accident, and they never wanted me. They put me in a boarding school as soon as I was old enough to go. That's why I tried to stop Kevin's father from sending him." She blew her nose into a tissue and carried on, "It breaks you, you see. The lack of love breaks you."

I stayed still. I didn't want to interrupt whatever this was. A confessional or an unburdening. I was just grateful to be there, to be trusted enough.

"I know I'm not well. I have pills I take that make me feel better, that help me sleep, that help me get through the day. He knows it too. But these days I can't find them. My pills. He keeps moving them. He knows…" She gulped. "He knows that if I don't take them, I lose control. Everything," she waved her hands, "Everything spins off axis. I feel like someone else. Voices whisper in my head. They tell me to do things. You know?" Her blue gaze penetrated me. I took her hand in mine and said, "I know, Karolina. I do know."

At that moment, I felt as if we were one. Two sides of the same person. I had never felt closer to anyone else. Not Mami, not Jen, not any of my buddies from the army. Maybe she felt the same. She squeezed my hand with hers and let it stay in my clasp.

I wouldn't see her for another four months.

I found the coat in a dumpster. It was navy Cashmere, and the only thing wrong with it was a torn pocket. But for rich people, that was enough to throw it away. It was my lucky day. I came across it while rooting around for newspapers to line the little, forgotten doorway I'd found between 52nd and Fifth. It had served as a home for the past week, and now, with this coat, I could survive another month there.

Jonas had been missing for the last few weeks, and I had started to worry about him. Had he gone the same way as the others? As drifters, we had no friends. Our lives were too aimless, too reliant on food and shelter or the charity of others, to really form or keep bonds. But the streets were mean to people like us, and a few kind words, a nod, an acknowledgement that yes, we did exist, meant something.

Dreams of Karolina still ambushed me unexpectedly. That apricot blonde hair, those lips that sucked in nicotine greedily, those icy blue eyes. After Jen, she was the first woman I'd found myself attracted to. There was just something about her. An aura. As if she was one of us, but also not. As if she really belonged to another world and had only briefly stepped into ours. I desired her for sure, but more than that, I wanted to understand her. To figure out what made her tick. Our brief conversations had only left me feeling confused. Sometimes she would talk Proust to me, and other times, complete gibberish. It didn't matter. I just loved looking at her, listening to that soft voice, watching those lips move, and inhaling the sweet orange blossom smell of her. But I hadn't seen her in a long time. Where was she? Had she been to see Jonas? Had her divorce come through?

I missed her.

Looking at her, talking to her, I felt like there were still possibilities in life. There was still hope. She was so *clean*, so innocent, so devoid of any kind of artifice. I came alive when I was with her. My heart beat faster, the blood rushed quicker through my veins, everything seemed brighter. I forgot all the horrors of my past.

My God, I missed her!

Where was she? Did she even think of me? Did she miss me? Had that moment with her—that moment when I felt we were one—been just in my imagination?

The cops who turned me out the next afternoon asked me where I'd stolen the coat from. Then they took it from me. With the coat and my hideout gone, I went to Central Park and watched the horse-led carriages go by. Tourists and honeymooners enjoying the best of New York City, while their eyes glazed over the worst. Sometimes I wondered about the point of my existence. What did I contribute to the world? What was I good for? All my best years were behind me. All the hope and promise of my young life had been destroyed in a war of someone else's making. Then why did I still shuffle about on this planet? Who was I living for? Who would notice if I wasn't around? Maybe I needed to find a way to end it, too.

"How many more months, Marty?" Jonas dropped down on the bench next to me with a grunt.

I couldn't speak for a moment, the lump in my throat too large to swallow.

"One," I said eventually.
"So, after Christmas?"
"Yeah."
"You holdin' out okay?"
"Yeah."

How could I tell him that moments ago I'd thought of ending it all?

"Where you been, Jonas?"

"Around." He pulled out a cigarette, lit it and coughed as he took the first drag. "My daughter came to get me."

"Oh?"

"I didn't wanna go."

"Why?"

"No good being somewhere the folks don't really want ya."

"But you said…"

"Outta duty, man! She said she was only doin' it outta duty. I ain't some charity project. I'm her Pops."

His voice quivered on the last bit. I heard the pride and the hurt. I understood.

We sat in silence for a bit. Then he put his hand on my shoulder.

"You a good man, Marty. Don't ya forget it."

Then he ambled off, and I watched him leave as the horses neighed in the background.

※

The leaves had turned golden, then russet, then black before falling to the ground. Soon the branches would be bare, and the birds would have flown south to warmer climes. Sometimes I wished I could sprout wings and fly away, too.

I was back to reading the first Harry Potter book, the one in which Hagrid, the giant, arrives to take Harry to the wizard school. I felt as small and frightened as Harry. My goal was nearer now, but seemed so far away. There were times I wondered if I'd make it. Times when I wanted to return to the oblivion of alcohol once again. But some wilful stupidity made me believe that better things lay ahead, even if the voices in my head said that I deserved to die like a rat in the sewers.

The flashlight wavered in my hand as I tried focusing on the page. It was too cold to concentrate, the chilly wind penetrating the layers of clothing I wore.

"Marty?"

It was barely a whisper, and I almost ignored it. But something made me look up, and there she was. Karolina. Her alabaster skin glowing in the twilight, fur coat on, diamonds twinkling at her earlobes. A mirage or reality?

She sat on the step next to me.

"What are you reading?"

I showed her the cover of my book.

"Oh," she said, her glossed lips parting. "What's it about?"

I just stared at her, but she was already pulling out a cigarette, offering me one, then blowing smoke rings into the air.

"I got divorced."

"I heard."

"Who told you?"

"Jonas."

"Hmm." She smiled as she looked at me. "I have a room at The Plaza. You want to come?"

Speechless, I kept staring at her.

"Come on!" She stood up suddenly, waiting for me as I scrambled to gather my belongings.

We walked there in silence. I wasn't sure what she wanted from me, but if I could get a hot meal and a warm bed for one night, I could salvage enough hope for the next few weeks.

And then there was her. Just being with her felt like a miracle.

The doorman to The Plaza saluted her smartly before clocking who she was with. Then he barred the entrance.

"Mrs Gottesman, you know you can't…"

"Bernie, let me through!"

She spoke calmly, softly even.

"But Mrs Gottesman, I have my orders."

He stood firm, not allowing her to move any further.

Then, with a loud shriek, Karolina sank to the floor.

"I am NOT moving! Let me in, I tell you, or I will call the police."

Other guests and passersby stopped to stare as she continued to scream and cuss, hysteria making her sentences unintelligible. The doorman looked around, then indicated to someone inside before moving to allow us in.

Once inside, three security guards immediately whisked us to a small brown door that led to the back offices.

The manager, a tall thin man with a name badge that read "Mr Wolf" stood up as we were brought into his large office.

"Mrs Gottesman," he uttered, staring down his nose at Karolina.

"Joe, they won't let me go to my room!" Karolina had streaks of mascara running down her face, her hair escaping from the French chignon, her hands trembling as she stared up at the manager.

A flicker of something resembling pity crossed his face before the shutters came down again. Before he could say anything, I spoke up.

"Mr Wolf," my voice came out hoarse. "Sir. If this is about me, I am happy to leave. Mrs Gottesman was just bein' charitable, is all. I am sorry, sir. I should never have come…"

His eyes flicked to me, then flicked back to her.

"Mrs Gottesman. You have been banned from entering the premises. Bernie should have known better. Now, security will escort both of you out from the rear entrance. Please do not return or I will have to take stricter measures."

She mewled like a kitten, almost collapsing on me. The manager pulled out a chair and called for a bottle of water for her. He addressed me then.

"Are you her friend?"

I nodded. I wasn't sure what I was, but I was here and, by my reckoning, she needed me.

"Mrs Gottesman stayed with us for over a month, but she hasn't paid her bill and I don't think she can, either. Mr Gottesman is a valued patron, and we have consigned this to a bad debt. However, we cannot allow her or you," his nose quivered as he looked me up and down, "anywhere near our establishment." He shut his eyes briefly, then reopened them and spoke again, softly this time. "She needs help. If you are a friend, get her some help."

Much after he'd put fifty dollars in my hand and ushered us out, I took her to Bryant Park. The skating rink was up and the Christmas stalls were twinkling with baubles and knick-knacks. The hot dog seller was doing brisk business as people lined up to fill their already full stomachs. The air felt smoky, as if the haze of our lives had lifted up into the atmosphere and blanketed it.

"You hungry, Karolina?"

She shook her head, burrowing deeper into her coat.

I went and got us two hot dogs, careful to put the change away where no one could get to it.

She ate, wordlessly. Then we watched the skaters together.

At night, we went back to my hideout and covered ourselves with her fur coat, falling asleep in each other's arms.

In the morning, she was gone. She'd left me her fur coat but taken one of my Harry Potter books. The third one. What would she do with it? I wondered how I could track her down. I folded the coat as small as I could and shoved it into my knapsack, before going in search of Jonas.

He was sitting outside Macy's again, holding up his sign.

"Karolina came to see me yesterday," I said, as I sat down next to him. A kid on a skateboard nearly ran over my leg, but I pulled it back in time.

Jonas looked blankly ahead, not acknowledging me.

"Hey, man! You ok?" I asked.

"You got no right," he muttered.

"What?"

"You got no right to be sleeping with her."

Word got around, even on the streets of Manhattan.

"Jonas, we didn't do nothin'. We just slept."

He looked at me then, and I glimpsed a peculiar expression.

"Look, man," I pleaded with him. "She's out there somewhere, and she ain't doin' good. We need to get her to her family or someone who can help her. You know her better than I do. Tell me where I can find her."

Jonas stared ahead again, his lips pursed, his head moving side to side.

"They don't want her," he said, finally. "She tried going to her sister in San Francisco, but the sister didn't want no loony tunes, she said. So she came back."

"But surely she got something outta the divorce? Why is she on the streets?"

"She got nothin', Marty. The husband put all his money and stuff overseas, and Karolina…" He puffed his cheeks and blew air out from his mouth. "She's smart, but she's also like a kid. Ya know?"

I nodded.

"She wasn't smart enough for him. He turned her out with nothin' but that fur coat."

I stood up.

"We need to find her, Jonas."

He looked up at me, his eyes sad.

"Last I heard, she was near Hudson Yards. She gave her earrings to some poor jerk in the morning. Later she traded her watch to Billy Ray for his pack of smokes."

I thought of her in that blue sweater and jeans, wandering around in the cold, headed to who knew where. A prickle of fear ran down my spine.

"I gotta get to her."

"It's too late, Marty. No one can get to her no more."

Jonas looked down at his feet and I saw her socks on his ankles.

My heart racing, I ran as fast as I could, my breath coming out in smoky puffs.

Run, Marty, run. The voices in my head screamed at me as I ran.

In training, they'd made us carry heavy duffel bags and run obstacle courses. Today felt no different. I ran around people, jogged around delivery trucks, nearly tripped over a loose metal grate, but recovered and kept running. Nothing mattered anymore. Not the weight on my back, not the sweat pooling under my armpits, not the worn heel of my left shoe that sent shards of pain up my leg. All that mattered was getting to Karolina. Finding her before she disappeared.

"I want to disappear," she'd whispered in my ear before we fell asleep. "I want to evaporate like a droplet of rain."

I had thought she was being poetic, her softness melting into my wiry body. I'd wanted her so much at that moment, but held back, knowing it wasn't fair. Now, I wish I'd paid more attention to her words and not her body.

※

I remember when they'd first unveiled the Vessel to the public in 2016. Hundreds of people had gathered at the event, including Bill de Blasio, the Mayor. Its honeycomb-like structure was meant to rival the Eiffel Tower in France. The copper clad steps invoked the child in everyone as they climbed and explored the gigantic jungle gym.

Today it gleamed red-gold in the pale, watery late morning sunshine. Tourists were already lining up to climb it, to be photographed outside it, to take back a memory of Manhattan to their parts of the world. New York City was as much a place of dreams as it was of hard and gritty reality. Those who came from outside they took a bite of the juicy Big Apple, never eating enough to taste the core that was moldy and rotten in parts.

I looked around frantically. Was she here somewhere? She would have to buy a ticket to get inside, and she had no money. Maybe I could steer her back to my little hideout, talk sense into her, tell her about the place I was gonna get. A place where we could live together, make a life together.

When I was a little boy, I had watched a movie with Mami. It was called 'Vertigo' and the woman in it, Kim Novak, reminded me of Karolina. Tall and beautiful, but remote. Cut off from the rest of the world, living inside her own head. It didn't end well for Kim Novak in the film.

Where was she? Where was Karolina?

I jogged around; the knapsack bouncing on my back. I was sure she had headed here. In one of our brief and lucid conversations, she had mentioned how she'd been here for the unveiling with her husband, a very important citizen of NYC. They had laughed and mingled with the other guests, and drunk champagne, marveling over the idea of the Vessel. But he, Mr Gottesman, had never brought her back to see it properly. He had never allowed her to climb it like a child or explore it like an adult. It was something she had always regretted.

My instinct had brought me to this copper structure. I hoped this was where she had been headed when someone had spotted her near Hudson Yards. My heart beat furiously in my chest and I panted as I ran around the perimeter of the Vessel. Security wouldn't allow me to get any nearer. The guards looked at me suspiciously as I tried peering through the hordes to see if I could spot her.

"Hey! You. Yeah, you." One of them came towards me, his arms tight with tension, hands curling into fists. "Whatchu doin'? Why you botherin' these people?"

I backed away. This wasn't the time to get into a fight. All I wanted was to find her and tell her that she meant something to someone. She meant something to me.

There was no sign of her. Not in the rapidly swelling crowds of people who had braved the cold to come admire this architectural behemoth.

"Fancy words!" I heard Jonas' voice in my head. "You usin' the fancy words again, Marty?"

What good did my fancy words, my love for reading, my being smart get me if I couldn't tell a woman what I felt?

I circled around the Vessel again, trying to spot a tall blonde in a sky blue sweater and rhinestone encrusted shoes. Where was she?

Maybe I had been mistaken. Maybe she hadn't come here at all. I racked my brain as to all the places she could have gone to. Nearby places. There was the mall, but I couldn't imagine her wandering there, penniless and befuddled. Then there was the observation deck on The Edge. But would she be allowed up there in her state?

Love had no logic. It could strike the richest or the poorest in an instant, like a bolt of lightning. Here I was, a bum, a homeless vagrant in love with a woman who was so out of my league it was laughable. Even if I could imagine a future with her, could she with me? And what of her mental health? Could I afford to keep her safe and medicated enough to function normally?

But what was normal?

Who was normal?

These people rushing around, queuing up, traveling from afar. Were they normal? Did they have it all sorted in their lives? And if not, why did we compare ourselves to them? Was Karolina or I any less deserving of love just because we weren't one of them? So what if we existed on the edges of civilized society? Could we not carve out a tiny space to live and love?

All these thoughts circled in my head like vultures. They were moot. First, I needed to find her.

Suddenly, there was a shriek. Someone screamed.

"Oh, no! She's jumped. Oh my God!"

The crowds separated and coalesced again, and the security guards ran towards the screams.

My blood ran cold. This was what I had feared. This was why I had run all the way here. Had she done it? Disappeared? Launched herself off the Vessel like an eagle eager to splatter herself on the concrete below?

I ran again, towards the noise and the crowds. I didn't care who tried to stop me now. I'd fight them; I'd fight them with my bare fists if I had to.

Police sirens sounded in the distance. 911 had already been called. My Karolina. My poor, poor Karolina. Would they scrape her off the pavement like the garbage she had thought she was? Who would claim her? Who would want her except me? And even I wouldn't be able to put her back again. Not in the way I had wanted to.

SIX - STRANGE STORIES OF LOVE

Gasping for breath, I pushed my way to the front. I had to say goodbye. Even if it was in this gruesome and grisly manner.

It took me a minute to focus on the woman who was splayed on the floor, blood spreading out in a thick pool around her. On the dark hair, the burgundy dress that had ridden up to reveal the black stockings; on the knee-high boots distorted horrifically on the grotesquely misshapen legs. I backed away from the sight, still trying to catch my breath.

Not. Her.

Not. My. Karolina.

The trembling started suddenly; the sweat cooling on my body, the sub-zero temperature reminding me where I was and who I was, again. Moving away from the crowd, I went to sit on a bench near the Shed. With its roof resembling a large white garbage bag that moved in ripples, it was meant to be a building that shifted and adapted to the artists and the works it housed. Barely anyone walked past me now. Everyone had rushed to the scene of the tragedy. I could hear the ambulances arriving, the premises being cordoned off; the people being shunted away. I didn't turn to watch. There was nothing to see.

There was the smell of toasted acorns in the air, of rich folk readying themselves for Christmas. There were thick and heavy clouds in the sky now, obscuring the sun. Clouds pregnant with snow that would fall later. The tree branches were bare of leaves but festooned with twinkly lights that would glow as the darkness fell. The city was preparing itself for the festive season. Year after year, Christmas came and Christmas went. Babies were born and people grew old. Some died from natural causes, others decided that life on this earth was just not good enough.

What drove a person to suicide? Desperation, anger, futility? I had felt all those emotions at one time or another. There were times when I had wanted to end it all, too. But now, suddenly, it felt like a copout, an excuse to bow out early. Father Escamilla had once told me that life was the most precious gift that God had given us, and it was not for us to decide when to finish it.

I had finished many lives in my time. That, in turn, had nearly finished me. As I sat there, my heart still beating unevenly, I figured it was time to forgive myself. It was time to live again. I had a purpose now, and that purpose went by the name of Karolina.

A complicated woman for whom I felt the most uncomplicated of emotions.

Love.

Would God give us a chance? Were we worthy of it?

I felt her before I saw her.

She sat down next to me, the sweet orange blossom scent of her wafting towards me, and then she put her head on my shoulder. I looked down at her shoes, rhinestones missing, socks donated to Jonas.

"Marty," she whispered, her breath coming out in a vapor, "I'm cold."

Wordlessly, I took her fur coat out of my knapsack and wrapped it around her.

We sat together in silence as the sirens blared behind us.

THE PURPLE RIBBON

"Do you believe in ghost stories?"

Andrew could hear the silent ripple of the water in the dark, and all he could see were the whites of Diego's eyes as he turned around to address him.

"That's a silly question!"

"Okay," Diego laughed, "let me ask it differently. Do you believe in love stories?"

Andrew sighed. He really didn't want to get into this right now, but Diego wouldn't let go until he'd needled enough answers out of him.

"Yeah, I guess. I mean, some. I believe in some love stories. Not all of them. Most are just people pretending to be in love."

Diego laughed even louder, his voice carrying over the dark waters of Xochimilco's canals as they walked side by side in the night.

"But why do you ask?" Andrew realized his voice had come out plaintive. He cleared his throat hastily.

"Because, my friend, I'm taking you somewhere different tonight."

"Different? But you promised…"

"No, no. I didn't promise. I said I would see what I could do."

Andrew knew he shouldn't have trusted Diego. Even back in

college, Diego had always believed he knew best; always done what he wanted to do. Not much had changed in the years since.

"Diego…"

"Shhh. Now listen, you don't say much. Let me do the talking, okay?"

Diego switched on the flashlight, and the faint light illuminated a small hut on the edge of the water.

"Where?"

Diego stopped and turned.

"Andy, do you trust me or not?"

Andrew wanted to shout "No." No, he didn't trust Diego one bit. Not since that night nearly five years ago. But what choice did he have? He was here, and this was happening.

"Uhhh… Sure."

"Then let me handle this. How much can you spare?"

"What?"

"How much cash can you spare, dude?"

"Two hundred pesos?"

"Not enough. Can you make it five?"

Andrew took the wallet out from his cross body satchel and counted the notes in the dim light that Diego shone on his hands. With five hundred pesos gone, he would barely have a hundred odd left. Would that be enough to get back to his hostel in Centro Histórico? Diego saw his hesitation and snatched the money out of his hand.

"Stop worrying, *güey*. We need the money now to convince the man."

What man? But Andrew let Diego take the pesos and followed behind him silently. He supposed he could always get Mom to transfer some money into his account. He didn't want to. As a twenty-five-year-old, he wanted more than anything to be independent. But his career as a documentary filmmaker had yet to take off. Once it did, though, he would pay everyone back. Mom, his sister Darleen, and even Gina.

"You need to stop dreaming, Andy!" Gina had said, face blank as she stared down at him. "Dreams don't pay bills."

Didn't he just know it?

Diego gave two raps on the door, then waited. There was some shuffling inside and a few minutes later, a wizened old man opened the door and peered at them.

Diego spoke in rapid-fire Spanish, only a few words making sense to Andrew. He heard island, boat, night. Was Diego actually following the brief? Then he saw the old man shake his head and try to shut the door. Diego inserted his foot in between and held up the sheaf of notes. The man responded in a low voice.

What was happening?

"That was Ángel," Diego said, leaning against a tree as they waited for the man to return.

"Can you explain what is going on?" Maybe the irritation he felt came through in his voice because Diego straightened up.

"It's okay, Andy. This is better. Much, much better than what you had planned."

"How? And what is this, anyway?"

Diego let out a tuneless whistle from his lips.

"Everyone knows about *Isla de las Muñecas*."

Yes, Andrew wanted to say, and that's why he was here in the southeast part of Mexico City, in Xochimilco. To visit the Island of the Dolls. He had wanted to film it at night, to see if there was any truth to the story of the dolls moving and speaking; of the spirit of the drowned girl haunting the island.

Legend had it that in the 1950s, a man named Julian Santana Barrera had found the body of a young girl at the bottom of the waterway just outside his door. She had drowned while out swimming with her sisters. Out of respect, Julian had taken a doll that was nearby, one he presumed belonged to the girl, and hung it up from a tree. But the spirit of the girl, plagued with sorrow, began to haunt him and the island. Julian found his crops failing, his island being preyed upon by ghosts, and when the altar he built to appease her spirit did not work, he began collecting dolls to protect himself. Over the years, he had collected more than a thousand dolls, hanging them up from trees, nailing them to buildings, and stringing them on clotheslines. Then he had died, leaving the island to a descendant who had chosen to not change a thing. The dolls remained, decaying and becoming creepier as the years progressed, until everyone swore that the island was truly haunted and no human could live there in peace.

Andrew had contacted Diego, knowing no one else in Mexico City, hoping his old college friend could find a way for him to film the island at night when the tourists had departed. Diego had said he would see what he could do.

Now this.

"I thought that's where we were going."

"We could have. I'd even found someone who would take us, bypassing the usual channels. Then I remembered Pacorro and the Island of the Ribbons—*Isla de las Cintas.*"

"What is that? I have never heard of it."

"Precisely, *mi amigo*! Few people outside of Mexico City have. In fact, even in Xochimilco, hardly anyone ever talks about it."

"Then how do you know of it, and what is it, anyway?"

Just then, Ángel returned and nodded to Diego. They followed him down the narrow path towards the flat-bottomed *chalupa* docked at the edge of the water.

"He wasn't happy to go there," Diego said as they boarded the *chalupa*, "but the pesos convinced him."

※

Ángel steered the *chalupa* silently through the dark canals. The only sound was the occasional slap of his paddle against the water.

"In the day Ángel sells snacks to the *trajineras* along these waterways," Diego said, inserting a stick of chewing gum in his mouth and offering a stick to Andrew, who shook his head in refusal.

He had come over the weekend to ride in one of those flower boats and been amazed at the celebratory mood of the tourists and locals who traversed the canals in the colorful *trajineras*. Floating food vendors, *Mariachi* bands, beer, tequila and quesadillas made up a fun party. But Andrew's interest had been on the island they had passed by, the decrepit dolls swaying gently in the wind.

At night the canals were silent, the parties having long departed. The only light illuminating the water was of the distant stars in the sky. The silhouettes of the trees on either side had taken on a sinister aspect, the hour of the night exaggerating every rustle, every murmur, every hiss into a sibilant threat.

"Where are we going, Diego? Where is this Island of the Ribbons?"

"Farther than the Dolls," Diego stretched his legs out in the narrow space of the *chalupa*. "And far more interesting than the Dolls."

"Why do you think that?"

"Because this island—*Isla de las Cintas*—is truly haunted."

How much of what Diego said was to be believed? He had always been full of far-fetched stories; outrageous claims and fabricated tales he'd passed off as God's honest truth.

"Tell me more."

"It is a small island, less than an acre, and has just one little hut on it. Pacorro lives there."

At the sound of the name, Ángel turned and muttered something in Spanish.

"What did he say?" Andrew asked Diego.

"Oh, he said, *loco*."

Even Andrew knew *loco* meant crazy. Who had Ángel been referring to? Pacorro or them?

Diego carried on.

"Pacorro must be a hundred years old," he laughed. "Okay, okay, I exaggerate. He must be eighty, at least. He has lived on that island for over sixty years."

"Why?"

"Ah, now that's what the entire story is about." Diego chewed on his gum for longer before continuing. "When Pacorro was nineteen years old, he fell in love with Fernanda, a rich man's daughter, who was only fourteen. He courted her with flowers and little notes, cornered her on the way to church, stood under her window daily, until she began to reciprocate his affections."

"Fourteen!" Andrew gasped.

"It was a different era, *güey*. Romeo and Juliet were only sixteen and thirteen when they met. Back then, these things didn't matter." Diego shrugged. "Anyway, Fernanda was the youngest daughter in the family, with five older siblings, two of them being girls of a marriageable age. They did not look upon their sister's love with kindness. In fact, you could say that they were jealous. Of her beauty, of her popularity, and of the fact that she had snared a suitor before them. A handsome young suitor, albeit not a rich one."

Diego trailed his fingers into the water.

"Did you know that there was a time when you could see right to the bottom? The water was that clear."

Andrew shook his head, then murmured a low no. He was impatient for Diego to continue, but knew from experience that if he displayed his impatience, Diego would take even longer getting to the point.

"How do you think Barrera saw the girl's body?"

"Which girl?"

"The one whose spirit haunts *Isla de las Muñecas*. Did you know he died in the very spot he found her all those years ago?"

"No, I didn't know that." A shiver went through Andrew.

"Spooky, right?" Diego flashed another white grin at him. "Don't worry, we aren't visiting her spirit tonight. It'll be another one you'll meet."

"Diego?"

"*¿Si?*"

"Do you believe in ghosts?"

"Everyone in Mexico believes in ghosts. It is part of our DNA. We celebrate the dead in *Dia de los Muertos*. I have gotten drunk on enough pulque to *see* ghosts, my friend!" Diego chuckled.

"Do they scare you?"

"Ghosts? Nah! What can they do to us, hey? We are solid, we are living. They are as thin as the air around us." He flicked some water into the air. "What can they do to us?"

Ángel muttered something again. Diego laughed and responded.

SIX - STRANGE STORIES OF LOVE

"He thinks I'm being disrespectful to the dead. I am not. I have a lot of respect for the departed souls of our ancestors. It's the ones that hang around, causing mischief that I don't much care for."

"Does Ángel understand English?"

Diego glanced at him. "A little. He has met enough *gringos* like you."

"Do the spirits on this island of… of… ribbons cause mischief?" Andrew tried steering Diego back to the main story, hoping he would take the bait.

"Spirits, no. One spirit. That of Fernanda."

"She died?"

"Oh, yes. But not before suffering."

"What happened?"

"Well, like I said, the sisters were jealous. So, they told their father, a rich merchant who had profited in the revolution by always being in the right place at the right time. The father had many grand plans of installing his daughters in rich and politically hefty households, thus securing his own position in a country that was emerging out of the unrest of revolution into relative stability. A penniless peasant courting his daughter was definitely not part of the plan."

A frog croaked nearby and Andrew jumped.

"These are night sounds, Andy. Xochimilco is a natural habitat for so many species of wildlife. This is their home. Why do they scare you so much?" Diego's tone was mild, but Andrew knew beneath it lay a taunt. The taunt of cowardice, of fear; a mocking of Andrew being chickenshit.

"They don't. I'm just not used to the sounds. City boy, after all," Andrew laughed self-deprecatingly. "So what happened then, to Pacorro and Fernanda?"

"The usual. Fernanda was locked away, Pacorro was threatened, and the rest of the household carried on as normal. But they had not reckoned for the lovers' tenacity. Where Pacorro was brave, Fernanda was resourceful, and between them they worked out a plan."

"What kind of plan?"

"Of eloping, of course. What other plans do lovers make?"

Once again, Andrew felt like an idiot. How could a mere twenty-four hours in Diego's presence reduce him to a stupid jerk again?

❧

"So, they eloped?"

"With some help from Fernanda's nanny. Now, this woman had grown up tending the *chinampa* farms of Xochimilco before graduating to becoming a housemaid and then a nanny. She knew it would be the perfect place for the lovers to flee to."

"Why was she helping them? Was she not worried about her job?"

"How could she not help them? Pacorro was her nephew, after all. Blood is thicker than water, *güey*."

So it was. Mom had said that to him once, and Darleen had shown it over and over again. Andrew realized how lucky he was to have such strong and loving women in his life. He needed to call them as soon as this adventure was over, to tell them how much he loved them, how much they meant to him, and how appreciative he was of their support despite his multiple screw-ups.

"They left in the middle of the night and the next morning there was pandemonium at the merchant's house. He called in all his powerful contacts to trace his missing daughter, vowing to have Pacorro's head on a stake. No one knew of the nanny's role or her relationship with Pacorro. It was a secret that the servants kept from their loathsome master. The police searched high and low for Fernanda and Pacorro; for months their posters adorned the pillars of Polanco and the neighboring areas. But the early 1940s were a time of upheaval in Mexico. Alliances were shifting, new politicos emerging, and a missing girl soon became a forgotten girl. Even the merchant realized it was best to let the story die naturally. He had two other daughters to wed, he had business connections to forge with America, he had sons to appoint as heirs. Fernanda became a footnote."

"That easily?"

"Not easily. It took months before the lovers could come out of hiding, but yes, soon enough it was all right for them to live openly in Xochimilco."

"Then what happened?"

"Look!" Diego pointed in the distance. "There is *Isla de las Muñecas*. We will pass by it shortly."

A hush fell over them as Ángel navigated the *chalupa* past the island, the bamboo fence distinguishing it from the other fake island set up to scam naïve tourists. A ripple passed over the water and Andrew thought he heard a little girl's laugh in the wind. Whispers crowded his mind suddenly—loud, argumentative, incomprehensible. He bent his head to hide his discomfort from Diego. Was all this only in his mind, or was he picking up the ghostly messages being transmitted from the island?

"Scared, Andy?" There was the slightest trace of a challenge in Diego's voice, and Andrew raised his eyes towards the island. But before he could say anything, Ángel spoke again. He sounded angry, his words running into each other, his paddling more ferocious, taking them past the island quickly.

"He thinks I am too arrogant, that I need to understand that spirits do not forgive people who mock them."

Andrew didn't speak. What had brought him here? Not a belief in ghosts, for sure. He had hoped that a documentary about the island would expose what centuries of superstitions and unfounded fears could do to people. Now he wasn't so sure. Maybe actually being here in the middle of the night, listening to all the strange sounds and feeling the peculiar *frisson* in the air, made him less of a non-believer?

"How much farther?"

"Not that much. Another half hour, I think," Diego answered.

"What happened to Fernanda then?"

"Ah yes, Fernanda. When the lovers emerged from hiding, she was six months pregnant."

At Andrew's sharp intake of breath, Diego turned around and grinned at him. "Did you think they were playing *lotería* all that time?"

He turned his back on him again and continued.

"Fernanda was a slight little girl with narrow hips. It soon became clear to the women in Xochimilco that a natural birth could prove dangerous for her. They advised Pacorro to get a medical doctor, as no *la partera* could manage a complicated birth."

"But, of course, Pacorro had no money. How could he go to a medical doctor? That was when he devised his foolhardy plan."

"What kind of foolhardy plan?"

"Pacorro was a trusting sort of fellow. He thought that by now Fernanda's father would definitely have forgiven his daughter. So, he decided to appeal to his mercy. He went without telling Fernanda. He left her in the care of the women of the *pueblo*, promising to return as quickly as he could."

"Then?"

"Well, weeks turned into months and Pacorro did not return. Frantic with worry, Fernanda insisted on going back to the island on which they had hidden."

"The Island of the Ribbons?"

"Precisely. There she waited and waited and waited for Pacorro."

"Where was he?"

"Where do you think? Thrown into a dungeon, of course!"

"Poor Pacorro."

"Poor Fernanda, more like. Half insane with grief, she took to tying ribbons all over the tiny island. Ribbons that she had used to adorn her hair were on branches and stems, while her own hair became loose, wild and matted."

From the front of the boat, Andrew heard Ángel let out a deep sigh.

"The women from the *pueblo* tried to convince her to come with them. They tried to tell her they would help with the birth, but she didn't want to listen to reason. She insisted she would wait for Pacorro, that he would be back soon; he would be back in time."

Diego halted his story, cleared his throat, then carried on.

"She died waiting, trying to give birth on her own. It must have happened at night. No one heard her screams, no one found her in time."

Goosebumps rose on Andrew's arms as he pictured the scene.

"A few days later, when the women visited with supplies, they found her and the baby, rotting in the heat, being feasted upon by flies and buzzards."

Diego ran a hand over his face.

"They buried the bodies, marking the place with a few rocks and a stick on which they tied the last of her ribbons: a purple one. That way, they hoped that when Pacorro returned, he would know where his wife and son were buried."

Diego fell silent. The only noise was the occasional splash of the paddle and Ángel's low mutters. After a few minutes had elapsed, Andrew asked, "When did Pacorro return?"

"Nearly three years later. When Mexico became an active belligerent in the World War in 1942, it agreed to contribute hundreds of thousands of temporary farm and railroad workers to the United States under the Bracero Treaty. That's when a lot of the non-violent offenders were released, Pacorro amongst them. He fled almost straight away to Xochimilco, hoping against hope finally to meet up with Fernanda and his baby."

Ángel docked the *chalupa* on one the side of a small island.

"Ah, we are here!" Diego declared. "Ready for some action, Andy?"

As they stepped out onto dry land, Ángel grabbed Andy's sleeve and whispered, "Do not be afraid to run, *señor*. I wait here for you."

He pressed something small and metallic into Andrew's palm, then withdrew into the safety of his little boat almost at once.

※

The silence was oppressive. This was no island of whispers and complaints. No dolls swayed in the breeze. Even the wind barely breathed in these overgrown thickets. This was an island of abandonment and death. Dark, dreary, bleak from what little Andrew could make out in the dim light of the half-moon.

Diego's flashlight cast a pale glow on the narrow path they were treading.

"Where are we going, Diego?" Andrew whispered, his rucksack suddenly feeling heavy with the Sony DV camera he was carrying.

"To Pacorro's hut," Diego replied, not bothering to lower his voice.

"Have you been here before?" Andrew raised his voice to a notch above a whisper, trying to calm his jangled nerves. Fernanda's story was still circling in his mind, and just a moment ago, he thought he'd seen a pale ribbon tied to a branch, but just as soon as he'd glimpsed it, it had disappeared.

"In the daytime many years ago. No ghosts spotted then, but Pacorro informs me she is real." Diego was cheerful, upbeat. Somehow, it didn't feel right.

"How do you know Pacorro?"

"Remember his aunt, the nanny? She was my *abuela*. Grandmother."

"You are related?" Suddenly Andrew wondered if this was some kind of elaborate hoax. He wouldn't put it past Diego. But just as soon as the thought crossed his mind, he felt an icy finger trace the back of his neck.

"Hey?!" He jumped, swinging around, wide-eyed.

Diego stopped and spun around, too.

"What's the matter? What happened?"

"Something… no, someone… just touched my neck." He shivered.

"So, Fernanda has said hello." Diego looked unconcerned. "Come. Let's go meet Pacorro."

Andrew wasn't sure what to expect when the door to the hut opened. Maybe he had been expecting someone like Ángel—old, balding, wiry, and bent over. Instead, a tall, rugged, sinewy man with a full head of entirely white hair stood in front of them. This was Pacorro? Wasn't he meant to be nearly eighty? This man looked nearer to seventy. But when he looked closer, he saw the deep lines grooved into his skin, the rheumy gray eyes that did not alight on anything for more than a second—moving, always moving, as if in search of something or someone.

"Hola, Pacorro! ¿Cómo estás?"

Then, without waiting for a response, Diego pushed in, indicating that Andrew should follow.

A sour odor hung in the air—unwashed clothes and poor ventilation—but the hut was tidy. A small stove sat in the corner, a cast-iron skillet on it. A few utensils, a chipped plate, and a small bottle of pulque were all that made up his kitchen. On the other end was a rough hewn bed covered with a sheet that had seen better days.

Diego kept up a steady stream of chatter and, at some point, Pacorro's eyes shone with a latent recognition. He nodded slowly, as if coming to some personal realization.

"I've told him you are here to film the island and to meet Fernanda," Diego translated.

"Is that okay with him?"

"Sure. Why not? He's always happy to have company."

Pacorro didn't look happy. He looked resigned.

"When you say *meet* Fernanda…?"

"Oh yes. She doesn't always declare herself. Quite a moody ghost she is. A woman, after all!" Diego laughed loudly at his own joke, startling Pacorro out of his reverie.

A croaky command issued from him, which stopped Diego's laugh mid-stream. Then Pacorro spoke slowly and at length. Andrew understood little of what he was saying, but his eyes followed every emotion flickering on the aged face. From sorrow to helplessness, from anger to despair. Diego took out his packet of chewing gum and offered one to each of them. They both declined. He carefully placed a stick in his mouth and turned to Andrew.

"He says that she has still not forgiven him. She goads him with visits and then disappears for days on end. Sometimes she is sweet and loving, and other times she wails in fury like a banshee. She only ever comes at night, but he cannot predict when, and he cannot predict what she will be like."

Andrew digested it all silently.

"Ask him, are her ribbons still around the island?"

"I could tell you that. Most of them frayed and fell away, but people kept bringing more in remembrance. The island is covered with them. The only original one is the purple one there in that corner."

"The one that...?"

"Yes, the one on the grave. That is the grave in the corner. Pacorro just built the hut around it."

Andrew looked at the little mound of rocks in the corner, the stick tilting out of it, a torn and faded ribbon faintly purple, still attached to the stick, and suddenly felt every bit of Fernanda's desperation and wretchedness.

"Remember Olivia, Diego?" Andrew watched his face as he asked him the unspoken, the unforgotten. Diego's mouth tightened slightly, but the rest of his face remained relaxed.

"Olivia? Yes, vaguely. Are you in touch with her?"

"Not anymore. I was, for a while."

Diego's eyes shifted. He didn't want to go there, Andrew could tell. Didn't want to revisit his past sins.

Pacorro spoke again, in a low mumble, and they were both momentarily distracted from the past.

"What is he saying?" Andrew's eyes flickered from Pacorro to Diego.

"He says that he can sense she will come tonight. There is something in the air. But he also says..." Diego stopped, took the gum out of his mouth, rolled it into a ball and stuck it to the mud wall, "He says she goes after the impure of heart."

"Goes after?"

"Exacts her vengeance. *La venganza.*" Diego shrugged. "First time I've heard this. I thought she only bothered him."

Andrew felt for the small metal piece Ángel had given, the one he had slipped into his pocket unthinkingly. Now he examined its shape with his fingers. It was as he had suspected: a crucifix.

"Exacts vengeance, how?"

"Don't listen to the ramblings of an old man. Let's set you up. It'll be light in a few hours and then you will have lost your chance."

"Will I be able to film her? She's a ghost, isn't she?"

"I don't know, *güey*. You wanted to film a haunted island, and I've brought you to one. The rest is up to you."

✦

Andrew pulled the Sony camcorder out of his rucksack and checked if it had enough charge. There wasn't much else to set up, so they sat and waited.

"Can you ask Pacorro something for me?"

"Sure."

"Why is he still here? Why doesn't he just leave?"

Diego asked and nodded as he listened.

"He asks where would he go? This is his home."

"But…"

Pacorro spoke again, words gushing out of him.

"He says there is nowhere else he would rather be. This is where his family is, this is where they lie. He has lived and will die on this island."

Andrew chewed on his lip. He looked at Diego.

"He really loved her, didn't he?"

"They don't call him crazy for no reason."

"And you?"

"Me?"

"You told Olivia you loved her, too."

Diego stared at him, his eyes like two pinpricks in the gloom.

"That was a long time ago, Andy. Why are you talking about it now?"

"Because being here and listening to their story has reminded me that true love does exist. Even if it isn't the sailing-into-the-sunset kind of love. But it was never true love for you, was it?"

"Listen *güey*, I know you had a *thing* for Olivia, and she chose me over you. Who cares? It's history now."

Somewhere outside, an owl hooted.

"Do you know what happened that night?"

"Which night?"

"The night you dumped her."

Diego shrugged. He hadn't cared back then; he cared even less now.

"She miscarried."

Andrew stared hard at him, all his suppressed animosity returning with a violence that surprised him.

"She miscarried *your* baby!"

Pacorro jumped to his feet suddenly, putting his finger to his lips and shaking his head.

"Shhhh…" he said, staring at the grave, a deep trembling taking hold of him.

Andrew switched on the camcorder, his own hands shaking. From fear of an unseen entity, or a loathing of Diego he had resurrected from the dregs of his memories? He wasn't sure which. All he could sense was a fresh charge in the air, as if all the atoms had suddenly started colliding haphazardly; scattering, recoiling, attracting, repelling, and creating an indefinable energy. The temperature dropped by many degrees, and his breath turned to vapor. He pointed the camcorder towards the rocks and the ribbon, waiting for an apparition, for something dramatic to happen. Instead, he felt an icy breath near his ear and a cruel, mocking laugh reverberated in his mind.

"She's here," Diego whispered, looking scared for the first time that entire night.

"Yes," Andrew whispered back, turning the camera around to capture something, anything. Instead, he got Pacorro on his knees, sobbing.

"Fernanda, *mi amor, perdóname! Llévame contigo. Te lo suplico…*"

"What is he saying?"

"He's asking her to forgive him… to take him with her…"

The door to the hut swung open, and a whoosh of icy air went past them. Andrew followed.

"Diego, are you coming?"

"No… no… I can't…"

Andrew didn't wait. He followed behind her. He wasn't sure where she was leading, but he stumbled behind, following instinctively, the camera jumping on his shoulder as it recorded jerkily. Recorded what? There was nothing to be seen. But he could feel her. He could feel her rage, her loneliness.

At last, they came to a stop.

Suddenly, the air was completely still once again. The red blinking light on his camcorder told him it was still recording. He heard a rustle behind him and turned slowly, the camera shooting.

There she was. As clear as moonlight. A waif of a girl with ribbons in her hair. She gave him a mournful smile, then pointed down at something. What was she trying to show him?

He walked towards her, towards the edge of the water, still recording, hoping she trusted him enough to let him film all of this, all of her sad yesterdays and cursed tomorrows. As he approached the water, he saw the reflection of three bodies in there. All three were floating on their backs, arms crossed on their chests, eyes closed. All three were dead.

Mom, Darleen, Gina.

"Noooo!"

The scream escaped him as he backed away, stumbling, and the camera fell out of his hand. With a screech, she was in his face, her eyes wild, hair streaming behind her. He grabbed the tiny metal crucifix in his hand and held it up, saying, "Oh God, forgive me. Forgive me, forgive me. Please, let it not be true."

She recoiled and tore away back to the hut.

In the distance, he heard Ángel calling, "*Señor, señor...*"

Andrew closed his eyes, took a deep breath, and tried to calm his wildly beating heart. He walked back to the edge of the water and looked again. Nothing. It wasn't true. He sank into the soft mud and let his breathing even out. Then he reached for his fallen camera. Could he leave? Did he dare? He shook his head and slowly traced his steps back to the hut.

The door was open, but when he went inside, only Pacorro was there, still on his knees, still sobbing.

"Where's Diego? Pacorro!" Andrew shook him by the shoulders. "Diego ¿donde?"

Pacorro shook his head.

Andrew went back outside. The first lick of light was seeping into the inky sky, charcoal edges blurring into the palest lemon.

"Diego?" he called out, scared for his friend. "Diego!"

A cry, not dissimilar to his own, came from twenty yards away. He rushed towards it and found Diego cowering under a willow tree. His face was wet with tears and he kept repeating "no, no, no".

"Diego, it's not real. Whatever you saw, it's not real. She's playing tricks on our minds."

Suddenly, Diego's eyes widened, and Andrew sensed Fernanda was behind him. He turned around and looked into her furious amber eyes. Setting his camera down, he raised both his palms towards her.

"Fernanda," he said in English, "no one means you any harm. We are sorry for all your pain and suffering. Please forgive us, all of us, for the sins we have committed against our mothers, our sisters, our daughters."

The words tumbled out of him, barely making any sense. Did she understand him, this Mexican girl from a different century? Her ghostly visage stayed expressionless, watching him, listening as he babbled on.

"You are a woman. You create life; nurture it. You are love, Pacorro's love, the mother of his child. Forgive him. He waits here for your forgiveness, to join you and your baby in the afterlife."

Were words enough to convince her vengeful spirit that perhaps it was time to let go, to move on? And where were these words coming from? Which deep well of knowledge was he drawing from? All he knew was that they were having some effect, as her sepulchral form retreated, ebbing away from them, taking all her wrath with her.

᠅

Andrew slumped down next to Diego under the tree, watching the sun rise slowly on the horizon. He put an arm around his friend's shoulder, holding him until his trembling had subsided. They sat like that for what seemed like hours, but was in fact only twenty odd minutes. Diego seemed lost and scared, helpless as a little boy. Andrew had never seen him this way. He didn't know what to say, so he let the silence stretch out.

Diego spoke eventually.

"She showed me my dead baby. Olivia's baby."

"Yes."

"Then she showed me my parents and little brother and sister."

Andrew nodded.

"How did she know?" Diego asked, his voice barely above a whisper.

"I don't know, but all she wanted was to hurt us. That's because she is hurting; has been hurting for over half a century. That's a lot of pain to carry for such a long time."

Diego sighed.

"You know, Andy, when I first brought you over, I didn't believe the story of Fernanda's ghost. I thought I'd have a laugh at your expense, get Pacorro to give you the same crazy version of events he'd been giving us, and then leave with a story to share with my friends over margaritas."

"I know, Diego."

"*Loco* Pacorro. That's what everyone calls him. But it's me. I am the *loco* one. I was arrogant and foolish, skeptical enough to put you in danger. I'm sorry. Forgive me, Andy."

"Forget it, Diego. Nothing to forgive. Let's go find Pacorro now. I cannot imagine how he has lived here for sixty years."

"Love."

"What?"

"That was the other thing he said to me earlier." Diego stood up, then leaned against the tree for support. "He said love wouldn't allow him to leave. No matter which form she came in, no matter how angry she was, he was happy to see her. He loves her even now, even after all these years. You were right, *güey*, true love exists, even if it isn't what we expect it to be."

They walked together towards Pacorro's hut. Inside, he was fast asleep, clutching the purple ribbon in his hand.

※

Later, as they sat in the *chalupa* heading back to the *embarcadero*, neither of them had the energy to say much. Ángel had taken one look at their faces and handed them a *serape* each to wrap themselves in. They sat in silence, lost in their thoughts, as Ángel paddled and muttered all the way back. Words like *'loco'* and *'fantasma'* floated back to them occasionally.

On their journey, they passed by the Island of the Dolls again. This time, there were no voices in the wind. All Andrew saw was a sad and decrepit collection of dolls, one man's futile attempt to ward off sorrow and misfortune.

"Diego?"

"Hmmm?"

"I don't think I'll make this documentary."

"Why?"

"Dunno. It just seems too personal, too sad. I don't want to expose it to the world. I don't want Pacorro and Fernanda's home to become just another tourist attraction, you know?"

"Yes, Andy, I get that."

Diego stared into the distance, his dark hair standing up in spikes on his head.

"What you said back there, to her, to Fernanda… about love and forgiveness… Do you believe it?"

"Yes Diego, I do. If I didn't, she would have known."

"Has Olivia forgiven me?"

Andrew stayed silent.

"I mean," Diego threw him a quick look, "will she forgive me? If I call her, if I apologize?"

"I don't know, bro. Only one way to find out."

Diego nodded and settled back into silence.

The sun had risen high in the sky when they disembarked from the *chalupa*. Andrew put the little crucifix and the last of his pesos in Ángel's hand and said a quick *gracias*. Ángel pressed the crucifix back in his hand and muttered, "*No señor, es para ti.*"

He took it, grateful and abashed, determined never to forget the kindness of a man he barely knew. Then he picked up his rucksack, flung it over one arm and walked towards the metro station alongside Diego.

He was ready to head home, to head back to the loving arms of Mom and Darleen. Perhaps even Gina, if she'd have him. He looked around one last time at the *trajineras* lined up to take tourists down the canals of Xochimilco. Someday he would return. Maybe he would come with his family, maybe he would come alone. But he hoped that whenever he did, Pacorro and Fernanda would have long departed, in love and at peace, together at last for all eternity.

A NEW PLACE

It's foggy when she opens her eyes. Fog as thick as the grey blanket Ma covered her in when she was younger.

"Jack," she would say, "it's *dreich* out. Warm yourself up, boy."

Ma.

Where is she now? What is she thinking?

She stands up and feels her way forward. This fog is nothing like she's experienced before. In Inverness, the *haar* would hang over the River Ness, rolling towards the land and the buildings until nothing but shadows remained. Cold, bleak, eerie.

This fog is like a hug. It smells a bit like candyfloss… and bacon. She gropes her way through it, feeling for something, anything, to tell her where she is. Where does one go after?

Ma always talked of Heaven and hoped she would meet her family there—her Mamy and Da, and her sister. Only this doesn't seem like the Heaven she talked of. There is no one here. It's quiet, except for the gentle lapping of water she hears in the background.

She walks towards the sound, hoping there will be someone waiting there. The fog clears a bit, and she sees a tree stump. Suddenly it feels important that she sits there, so she does. The fog lifts and Jackie finds herself sitting on a tree stump in the middle of a loch. She isn't scared. She left fear behind in her old life. But she is curious. What kind of world is this, where she can walk on water, where the fog hugs her and the air smells like her favourite snacks?

Sitting on the tree stump, she thinks back to the moment that brought her here. In the end, it wasn't as scary as she'd thought. Everything that had led up to it had been far, far worse.

They say your life flashes before your eyes in the last moments. All she had seen was Ma's face. Her eyes filled with tears, her mouth opened in a silent scream. It wasn't fair to her. None of it was. But sometimes the pain of hurting the person you love the most is still worth amputating the agony out of your own life.

What is she now?

A boy, a girl, an amorphous genderless soul?

Miss Joshi, the Indian teacher, had once said that the soul does not conform to the definitions of the corporeal world. That was before she got fired. But Jackie believed it. Hers was an ancient culture and there had to be some truth in the wisdom she had imparted so casually.

"Oh Jack! Why must you question everything?" Ma cried out most days.

Sometimes Avril would look up from her book, her grey eyes meeting Jackie's in a tacit understanding. Avril didn't question, she just did as she pleased. Ma tried with her, but it was Dad who fought. Fought his daughter, fought his wife, fought everyone around him, and then went out and got blind drunk.

Where was he now? What was he thinking?

And Avril?

Did they miss her?

❧

"He is in a coma," the nurse informs Agnes briskly. She can already see her eyes sliding away, looking towards another door in the long, grey hallway. Agnes is desperate to hold her attention, to keep her there.

"H... how long will he... she... be that way?"

"Difficult to say," the nurse's eyes are back on her, a glimmer of pity in them. "He lost a lot of blood and there was considerable swelling in the brain. The doctors had to induce a coma before his body started shutting down completely."

Facts. Facts stated so coldly.

Agnes cannot cry any more. The tears have been wrung out of her and she feels dry and empty, like a well with no water.

"But…" Agnes can no longer hold her. The nurse walks away, leaving her standing there alone.

Jack.

Her mind circles back to her child.

Why would you do this? Why would you do this to yourself? To me?

When Jack was born, Mamy had said to her, "Now, what a bonnie baby he is. Same red hair as Avril. This one will break hearts, Agnes."

Oh, how true!

She looks down at her chapped hands, the skin on her knuckles red and raw, split from the chemicals in the cleaning supplies. Normally she would apply a salve to them, ease the pain a bit. Today she wants them to bleed, to hurt. If only to remind her that she is alive. That her life, despite everything she has ever done, has been reduced to this moment, in this hospital. Alone.

As a girl she had always loved trains. Mamy had taken her from Inverness to Edinburgh on one. They had packed treacle pieces and cheese and onion crisps, and Mamy had told her stories of her childhood. In Edinburgh, they had walked and shopped and met Mamy's friend. On the way back, she had fallen asleep with her head in Mamy's lap.

They had never taken the train anywhere again, but that memory became her fondest. Her love for trains remained.

Maybe she passed that love on to Jack, who loved trains, too. She had bought him an old train set from the charity shop for his fourth birthday, and he had played for hours with it, unmindful of the missing pieces. It still sat under his bed, dusty and unused, but he would not part with it.

She had always planned that one day she would take Avril and Jack on a day trip to Edinburgh, the way she had gone with Mamy. But there was never enough time and never enough money. Clyde drank most of it away. And if she dared ask for some, he would answer with the back of his hand.

Why Jack? She wanted to scream. But she knew why. In her bones, she knew. Jack, her baby boy, had grown up playing with trains but wanting dolls, wearing trousers but trying on Avril's skirts. Jack, who on his fourteenth birthday, had asked if he could be called Jackie, please.

Oh, Jack. Please come back to your Ma.

❦

There is a gap in the water. Clear and transparent. It's like looking through a window. Now Jackie knows why it was important to sit on the tree stump. It gives her a vantage view of the proceedings below.

She is lying on a hospital bed, tubes attached to her arms, her leg in a cast, the other leg… gone. Her entire face is covered, except for her eyes and nostrils. Covered in white bandages, but for the blood that has seeped through, forming an orchid-like pattern on the side of her head.

So.

It wasn't clean. It wasn't quick. And she isn't dead. Yet.

Jackie had had a plan. She didn't want Ma to find her in her room hanging from a noose. She had wanted it to be over quickly, painlessly, in the least messy way possible. She had hoped that by the time it was done, it would be too late for anything except to mourn her.

But what a pig's ear she'd made of that, too.

Dad had always said she was a useless *eejit*.

"Dressing up in girl's clothes. Agnes, what a blithering *tumshie* you brought into this world!"

Ah, Ma! Are you out there praying for my recovery?

The window moves for her to see Agnes.

She is sitting on a chair in a long, grey hallway. She is alone, wringing her hands, then jumping up to walk towards the door marked 'ICU'. Trying to look through the glass pane, shaking her head, walking back to the chair and slumping into it. Her face is as grey as the walls of the hospital.

Where is Dad? Where is Avril?

She wants to shout down at her, "I'm okay, Ma. I'm not in pain anymore."

She opens her mouth but no words come out. Wherever this is, it is not a place she can do anything in, except to observe.

She was never much of a do-er, anyway. That was Avril. Breaking the rules, sneaking out of the window at midnight, smoking cigarettes, mixing vodka with her Irn Bru, then vomiting it all up in an orange mess.

Dad tried to discipline her, even took his belt to her once, until she caught it in her hand and stood eye to eye with him. He backed off then. Never hit her again. Maybe even respected her after that. Avril was like that. Fearless.

Jackie wasn't. She was like Ma. Soft. Given to tears. Oversensitive.

Dad knew he could do what he wanted with them. Say what he wanted. And it was never kind.

It wasn't like she didn't try to be good. She studied hard. She came home on time, helped Ma with the washing up. She was good in every way except one.

She had been given the body of a boy, but in her heart, she had always been a girl.

※

Does Clyde know? Agnes had told Mhairi next door to tell him. But what had she said in the confusion of the moment—hastily flinging on a coat and grabbing the keys from the table as the police car waited outside? What had she said?

He hasn't turned up yet. She's been here ten hours, and he hasn't shown. Why is she surprised? When has Clyde ever been there for her?

In nearly twenty years of marriage, she could count the times he had on the fingers of one hand. Mamy had warned her he was a *crabbit erse*, but she had seen nothing beyond his cheeky smile and brawny arms.

She looks down at her rough hands, clasping and unclasping them. Her hands had once been so smooth, like a baby's bottom. Her thoughts are scattering everywhere. Past, present, past again. The only thing she cannot contemplate is the future.

She looks in her bag once again to see whether her mobile is in there, but no. It's charging in the kitchen, dangling off a wire. Useless to her right now when she could have been making calls, informing people, asking for help, for support. But maybe it is best this way. This cross is hers alone to bear.

If only she had stood up to Clyde. Told him where to go when he turned on Jack. Told him he was the *eejit*, not her baby. That he was the pervert, not her child. It was true that she had not understood at first, either. Why would Jack want to be a girl? What did it even mean? But in the end, what did it matter? She had come around when Avril had explained it to her, gently, carefully.

And look now! Look where he was, her poor *bairn*!

Why hadn't she fought for him? Why hadn't she understood what he was going through? She was his mother!

Suddenly the tears are back, and she hunches over, her body rocking backwards and forwards as she sobs. Great, wracking sobs filled with misery and guilt. So much guilt.

"Ma?"

Her daughter is standing in front of her. Agnes stands up, then collapses into her arms.

"Avril... Avril... Jack..."

She is incoherent in her grief. Avril holds her, stroking her back, murmuring into her ear. For this moment, their roles are reversed. They stand together, locked in mutual anguish.

"How is she?" Avril asks, pulling away from her.

Avril is the only one who calls Jack Jackie. The only one who accepted without debate or discussion what Jack wanted.

"She…" Agnes takes a deep, shaky breath. "They say it isn't looking good."

"Who have you spoken to?"

"The doctor in the beginning," Agnes sinks into the chair and Avril sits next to her, her face pale. "Then a nurse a little while ago."

There are more people in the hospital now, doctors, nurses, paramedics, people rushing in and out. A thrum of life that was missing just an hour ago. It's nearly 8 a.m., and Agnes realises she has been here fourteen hours.

"He… she… is in a coma. They have induced it to allow the swelling to go down. The brain… you see… and… and… she… lost a leg…"

Agnes shudders, and Avril lets out a little cry. Then they sit together, side by side, wordless, but for the prayers they breathe for the fifteen-year-old child laying in the room beyond.

*

Gender identity. Gender conformity. Gender dysphoria.

All these definitions came much later. At first, it was as simple as wanting to play with Avril's dolls or dress up as Cinderella.

In this strange place where Jackie is sitting on a tree stump staring down at the world, she doesn't mind what pronouns are used for her. Somehow, here it doesn't matter. She realises instinctively that the body is just a garb for the deepest, truest self. The soul.

Yet, as she looks upon her mangled body, she knows just how much she hated it on earth. She wanted the softness, the supple roundness that her sister possessed, not the firm, wiry frame she had inherited. She wanted to rid herself of every marker that made her male.

But, at first, it was as simple as slipping on a dress.

Ma put up with it, laughing when she was a child, perplexed as she grew into a teen. She hid it from Dad as long as she could. But Clyde already knew in some part of him that this boy, this useless excuse for a man, wasn't the rough and tumble son he'd always wanted.

"Are ye a faggot, boy?" Dad had screamed at her, flecks of spit landing on Jackie's face as she shrunk against the wall. Only because she had failed to score a goal in a football game he'd insisted she join. A game she detested, was terrible at, but only played because it pleased Clyde.

Acceptance of self, Miss Joshi had said, was the first step to understanding oneself.

At seven, she knew she was in the wrong body.

At ten, she tried hard to push those feelings away.

At thirteen, she realised they would never go away.

She needed to accept herself, to understand what, if anything, was wrong with her, and then, if she could, explain it to the people who mattered.

In the world below, her breathing is shallow and her eyelids flicker as if in a dream. Why is she still there? And how is she here if she is also there?

Two doctors walk into the room and consult her chart. They talk in an undertone, and Jackie doesn't really care about what they are saying. She has no intention of returning to that body or that life.

But something is niggling her. A feeling as though she has forgotten to do something. Maybe that is why she is still around.

In this place that is neither Heaven nor Hell, she waits for the answer to come.

Down there, she watches as Ma and Avril hold each other up as they cry and speak in broken sentences. She wants to call out to them, but she doesn't know how.

Even in the letter she left under the pillow, she couldn't explain what had tipped her over the edge. All she could write was, *Sorry, Ma. I love you and Avril.*

She looks at her body in this strange place and realises that it is as thin as a vapour. Jackie can no longer make out whether she is male or female, a boy or a girl. She feels no pain and no guilt. She is merely an observer, an audience member watching a play. She is simply waiting for the curtain to fall.

"When did it get so bad, Ma?" Avril asks, her voice hoarse from crying.

"Not long after you left," Agnes answers, blowing into her sodden handkerchief. "You took most of it away from Jack, didn't you, my darlin'?"

They both know that they are talking of Clyde's wrath, his unprovoked attacks on his wife and children. His smashing of furniture when he couldn't smash a face in.

"Yes," Avril shudders. "I tried to protect her, in the only way I knew Ma. But I couldn't take it anymore."

"Nor should you have. It is I…" Agnes leans back in the chair, unable to complete the sentence without finally acknowledging aloud her own failure as a mother.

"No one blamed you, Ma." Avril squeezes her hand gently. "Johnny says it's a cycle of abuse, and when you're in it, you can't see it."

Johnny.

The name hangs between them.

Agnes had met Johnny just once when he'd come to fetch Avril. He'd seemed like a good lad, but she'd never had a chance to find out. Clyde had clobbered him on the street the following week for laying a finger on his daughter.

"No daughter of mine is seeing a darkie!" he'd glowered at Avril.

Avril being Avril, she'd packed her bags and left the following day. That was seven months ago.

"How is it, with Johnny?" Agnes asks, glad for a moment's respite; to take her mind away from Jack.

"Wonderful." Avril smiles a sad, sweet smile, all the fire in her turned to molten love. "Johnny loves and respects me, Ma. He listens to what I have to say and disagrees politely if need be. He knows I will never be treated like a doormat. Never! But he says that the women in his family are all strong and he's used to that. Believes that's how it should be, anyhow."

"Then you are a lucky lass," Agnes says, looking down at her scuffed shoes.

"We're engaged, Ma." Avril holds out her left hand, a tiny diamond sparkling on her ring finger.

"Ah." Agnes sighs, suddenly feeling even more alone.

"I wanted to tell you, but Dad…"

"Yes."

They sit in silence, each lost in their own thoughts.

The first doctor had said that Jack was lucky to be alive. Lucky that he'd got thrown forty feet into the air and then to one side when the train hit him. That was the only reason he had survived. Lucky? Agnes isn't sure that's how she would have put it. Yet she is willing to have her child back, no matter what condition his body is in or however long it takes for him to recover.

Irony comes in many guises.

There had been a conversation once when Jack had talked of something called gender reassignment. Of wanting to change his body to a girl's. She had brushed it off, saying she didn't understand any of it. Jack had looked at her, his eyes deep pools of hurt. She had looked away then, busying herself in the kitchen, refusing to give him what he wanted—a listening ear, a shoulder to cry on, someone he could lean on. More especially after Avril's departure.

"Why do you think she did it, Ma?" Avril asks.

Agnes takes a deep breath and turns to face her.

"Why do you think, Avril?"

❧

Jackie had been bullied all her life. From her father to her schoolmates, no one had spared her. Maybe it was her effeminate ways, her refusal to conform, her need to be *seen*.

It didn't matter that she was a polite, kind child. It didn't matter that she cared enough to volunteer at an old people's home. It didn't matter that she painted the most glorious sunsets over River Ness, her art teacher telling her there was a future there. All that mattered was that she was different. Othered even from the others.

She knew no one else like herself. Not in Inverness.

It wasn't until she started searching the internet that she found that there were so many more. Young boys, girls, men and women who came to be in bodies that were alien to them. Who wanted so much to be someone else. In America, a very famous athlete had lived her entire life being a man, before deciding in her sixties to transition to being a woman. She'd done it successfully and been accepted for it. Others had done it too.

Jackie stayed up late, night after night, reading articles on her phone about transgender people. What it meant to transition, what gender confirmation meant. At fourteen, she was perhaps too young. Could she hold out till eighteen?

Avril had been supportive all along, but even she balked at the idea of hormone treatment and surgery.

"Could you not live like a gay man?" she'd asked her once, on one of their long walks together.

"It's not the same thing!" Frustration made Jackie snap at her, something she regretted immediately. "I'm sorry."

Avril shook her head and smiled. "It's okay. Tell me more. I want to understand."

"You are cisgender, born into a binary world, conditioned to accept only two genders, and your identity is closely tied to your gender. Those two things are not separate for you, not in conflict." Jackie took a deep breath. "There are people who are non-binary. People who identify as a separate third gender, an intermediary one, or they have genders that fluctuate and they are gender fluid. That's why many people want to be referred to as 'they' rather than just 'him' or 'her'. They don't want to be confined to binary definitions."

Avril nodded her head and said, "But you're not one of them."

"No. I am what they call transgender. My gender identity differs from my sex assigned at birth. I am female, I feel female, I think and act like one, but my body tells me I am male." Jackie clenched her jaw and looked out over the water. "That is why it is important for me to try to change that. Otherwise, everything in my life will be a lie. A lie that I am living right now. I don't want to go into the future in the same way. I don't want to be sixty years old and filled with regret for the life I didn't get to live."

"How can I help?"

"Talk to Ma."

Avril nodded again, then turned to look at her.

"And Dad?"

"I will talk to him… when… when I can."

⁂

Agnes remembers the day well.

It was Jack's fifteenth birthday, and Agnes had saved up enough to buy the one thing he'd asked for, over and over again. A perfume from The Fragrance Shop. A girlie perfume.

On his birthday, she'd wrapped it in brown paper and tied a string around the box with a small card saying - *Darling Jackie, Enjoy your present. Ma.xx*

She hadn't wanted Clyde to see it. She had wanted to give it to Jack separately, before Clyde got home from work. With both Jack and Clyde out of the house, she'd baked a small sponge cake and put some jam and whipped cream on it. Her standard cake for all their birthdays. The children had always loved it. Besides, she couldn't afford anything fancier.

When the key turned in the lock, she fully expected it to be Jack returning from school. Instead, Clyde stood in the doorway, holding three packs of fish and chips. His eyes were bright, and his smile was cheery. He'd been drinking, she could tell, but only enough to put him in a good mood.

"Where's our Jack, then?" He came forward, holding up the brown paper packets that were leaking oil. "No need for cooking now, is there?"

He set it down on the table and she winced as the oil oozed on to her spotless tablecloth.

"What have we got here?" He picked up the present and gave it a shake, not noticing the little card that had fallen on the floor. Agnes put her foot on it, quickly dragging it under the table.

"It's Jack's present."

"We're doing presents now? Where did you get the money from?"

"I've been saving up. Just a few quid. It's nothing important, really."

Just then Jack walked in, freezing in the doorway as he saw his father home before him.

Clyde dropped the present on the table and turned to face him.

"Happy Birthday, boy! Fifteen now, eh? A big lad." Clyde grinned at him and pulled him into an awkward hug. "I brought us fish and chips. Look!"

"Thanks, Dad." Jack looked from his father to her, and back again.

With a tiny nod, Agnes brought out the plates, hoping Clyde would have forgotten the present.

They ate in silence, listening to the occasional loud burp Clyde let out, the radio playing pop songs from the '90s. The only music Clyde would tolerate in the house.

Avril had been gone six months by then, and her name was never mentioned before Clyde. Jack and Agnes would talk of her often, wondering how she was getting on, hoping for another phone call from her. But Clyde had decided on the day she'd left that she did not exist anymore.

When they'd finished eating, the room still reeked of fish and vinegar, so Agnes opened all the windows, then brought out a knife to cut the cake. She'd put a single blue candle on it, the same one that was recycled year after year on all birthdays. Before lighting it, she said, "Make a wish, Jack."

Jack closed his eyes, paused briefly before blowing out the candle.

Clyde slapped him on the back and said, "Good lad!"

Then they sank back into silence, eating the cake, thinking their own separate thoughts.

"Open the present, boy!" Clyde said suddenly, his eyes searching for the box he'd seen earlier.

SIX - STRANGE STORIES OF LOVE

❦

That was the worst Dad had ever beaten her. And even though Ma had tried to come between them, she hadn't been strong enough. She'd run away that night, run all the way to Avril's new home. But when she'd reached there and looked through their window, she'd known she couldn't spoil what she was seeing. For the first time ever, her sister looked happy. Truly happy.

They were doing the dishes together. She would wash and Johnny would dry. They would kiss from time to time.

Jackie stood to a side and watched them for a long time, then she turned around and went home.

Now, as she looks down at the body on the bed, she understands what's been niggling her. She needs to ask forgiveness. Jackie has hurt so many people by what she did... Ma, Avril, the train driver, the bystanders; anyone who was witness to her self-annihilation. She needs to make amends. She needs to acknowledge that this way, while being the only way for her, was perhaps not the right way at all.

Besides, she needs to say goodbye. Goodbye to those she loved, and those who loved her, goodbye to the body which was the source of so much pain for so many years, goodbye to that life and that world, both of which were unwilling to accept her for who she truly is.

She has to return.

The water window closes just as quickly as it had opened up. The smell of bacon has disappeared altogether. Now, she can smell the loch. A briny smell, one she remembers from her school visit to Loch Ness, when they had all pretended to spot the monster in the water, squealing in mock fear.

On the way back in the coach, she'd wondered whether the monster felt as lonely as her. Whether being different from everyone was enough to turn someone into a monster.

. . .

The young doctor who is monitoring her vital signs sees her fingers moving and her eyes fluttering. Excitedly, she calls out to her colleague.

"Patient seems to be waking up!"

"How can that be? We put him under..."

"Get his mother. She'll want to know."

There's so much hustle and bustle around her now. She feels strange re-entering her body, like an old, forgotten prison that houses terrible memories.

Someone is opening her eyelid and shining a light. Someone else is injecting her left arm. She wants to laugh. All of it seems so trivial now. This race to keep the human body alive. A body that is nothing but an outward expression of the internal, a vessel to take refuge in for a while before moving on to another place. A new place.

Ma has come in now. Avril is with her. She sees the shock on her sister's face and feels sad. This she didn't want, but her pain had blinded her to the consequences. There is no sign of Dad, but she is fine with that. Whatever they owed one another in this life, she's hoping they are done with it.

She cannot speak, but as Ma sits next to her, clasping her hand, Jackie hopes that the tiny squeeze she gives it conveys her remorse. *I love you, Ma. Despite everything, I love you. Please find it in your heart to forgive me.*

"Is this good?" Ma asks the young doctor. "Is this a good sign?"

"We think it is. It's the first time I've seen a patient come out of an induced coma in this way."

Avril looks down at her, her face anguished.

"Oh Jackie," she whispers, "not this."

She can't move, she can't say anything, but a tear trickles out of her eye too. She looks at her beloved sister, at the ring on her finger, at the glow in her cheeks, and tries to convey her sorrow and contrition. *I'm sorry, Avril. I never wanted to hurt you.*

Then, suddenly, a thought blossoms in her mind. *Yes! Yes, it's you I will return to.*

There are already the first stirrings of life in Avril's womb. Much too early for the soul to settle in yet. But when it's time, Jackie will be ready. This time she will come to parents who will love her, no matter what. This time, she will become the person she was always meant to be, amidst the people she was always meant to be with.

With that thought, Jackie closes her eyes and drifts away to her special place. The waiting room of deep waters, bacon and candyfloss.

"We've named her Jackie," Johnny says as he holds his beautiful newborn daughter in his arms. She has caramel skin and shocking red hair.

Agnes nods, pleased. She's been knitting all morning, finishing the last little jumper for her tiny granddaughter. Avril is exhausted from her twenty-hour labour, but triumphant too. She's done it with nothing but gas and air. As natural a birth as she could manage in a hospital. Avril, always the rebel. Wonder what her little *bairn* will be like as she grows up?

"Wish our Jackie was here," Avril says, wistfulness lacing her words.

Agnes feels her throat close up, and she stands up quickly to fetch her flask of tea. Eight months since she lost her baby and not a day goes by that she doesn't think of how things could have been different.

"How is the charity going, Ma?" Avril asks from behind her.

"Still a ways to go, but we are talking to sponsors. People who might help us financially."

"Our Jackie would be so proud. Helping other children like her find their way... Never knew you had it in you, Ma."

"Nor did I." Agnes thinks of the evening she threw Clyde out. How he screamed and shouted, and when she wouldn't budge, how much he grovelled. Never knew she had that in her, either.

"Here, hold your granddaughter, Agnes." Johnny hands her the baby and suddenly, there she is, this little miracle in her arms. She coos to the baby, letting her grasp her little finger. Just for a moment, the baby opens her dark brown eyes and gazes straight into hers. A jolt of electricity shoots through Agnes. *Could it be?*

Then, just as quickly, the thought dissipates as the baby begins mewling for her mother. Agnes sets her down on Avril's chest, watching her root for her mother's nipple, grab it greedily, and settle into contented suckling.

From somewhere, a thought floats into her mind—*Those that we love are never lost to us. They live on in our memories, in our daily prayers, in flowers and birds and babies. In all that is beautiful, and ugly too. For they are in everything we are and everything we do.*

She settles back into the chair, her heart lighter, her love for her family burning brightly; her way forward clearer than ever before.

LA DOLOROSA

Miguel revived the *zarzuela* in Spain. A dying art form that was only available on LPs was suddenly back in fashion because he, the genius of Spanish theatre, the *enfant terrible*, had brought it back from the dead.

When he cast Inés in the role of Dolores, the woman who had abandoned and been abandoned, her career was on the wane. She was still an incredibly beautiful woman, with her chiselled face and heavy-lidded eyes celebrated as the epitome of beauty, but she knew it was only a matter of time. The new, younger ones like Luisa Morales, Pilar Alvarez and Rita Tamayo were snapping at her heels, ready to take over the mantle of the most fêted theatre actress in Madrid. It was only a matter of time.

She didn't want it to bother her, but it did. Thirty-two years at the top had left her with little understanding of what it was like to live in anonymity. Or worse, obscurity.

At fifty, though, she was no longer the *ingenua* of the early years, and her days as the lead were numbered. Her own mother had graciously accepted the bit parts that came her way, eventually retiring without fuss to Seville. But Carmen had never really reigned supreme like Inés, much less been hailed for being *hermosa*, more beautiful than even the actresses who graced the silver screen.

Still, Inés did not set much store by her looks. She knew it was a happy accident, a genetic confluence of her father's fine-boned features and her mother's delicacy that had resulted in her beauty. It was a tool, and she utilised it as such. Her true calling was the art form—the imperative to perform and bring alive the works of literary giants and her forefathers. To act her heart out on stage and feel the immediacy of the audience's reaction. To hear the roar of approval and absorb each pin-drop silence of awe. To return for multiple curtain calls and shouts of *Bravo!* Yes, she came alive on the stage, her blood throbbing with the adoration of the thousands who gazed upon her week after week.

Inés had never married, still smarting years after her parents' acrimonious divorce. She did not see the point of it. Lovers were aplenty, and she always ended it sweetly, even with the ones who were bitter. In the end, all that mattered was that the time spent together wasn't tarnished by nastiness or anger.

A full life was all she had ever wanted, and it was what the Universe had delivered kindly into the palms of her hands.

So, to fall in love madly, to feel that deep, intoxicating *el amor* in the fifth decade of her life was too astonishing for words. And to formalise that love by way of marriage, an even greater astonishment. Perhaps, she reasoned with herself—as she looked at her husband standing at the altar, while walking down the aisle holding on to the arm of her eighty-year-old father—perhaps it was all in the timing.

Miguel was thirty-two when he asked to meet her. He was riding the crest of his latest success, a play with just two actors, no props, and the theme of existentialism. Hailed as the director who made theatre mainstream again, he was on the cover of every magazine, his dark, brooding looks only adding to his maverick allure. It would have been stupid to refuse. Besides, she was curious, too. What could he possibly offer her in his offbeat repertoire?

The *zarzuela*, as it turned out. A Spanish lyric-dramatic genre of yore that alternated between spoken and sung scenes. He wanted her for the part of Dolores in *La Dolorosa,* by the composer José Serrano. She was, he assured her, the only one who could convey the beauty and pathos of the jilted woman.

She was intrigued. Not so much by the role itself, but by the impassioned speech of the young man who ran his fingers through his hair unselfconsciously and spoke in a lilting voice that dipped at the end of every sentence, making her lean in to catch the words.

Their knees bumped every so often, sending an electric charge through her. Inés thought she was being silly, until she caught him staring at her lips as if he wanted to devour them, and her.

It was a success. Anything he touched turned to gold, and the fact that *La Dolorosa* was headlined by Inés Muñoz herself sent the cash registers ringing. When word got out that Inés and Miguel were to be married, *La Dolorosa* was given an indefinite extended run at Teatro Nuevo Apolo.

Those early years were heady. They were branded a power couple. Talented and beautiful, dark and fair, rich and glamorous, and completely besotted with one another. There were questions, too. About the eighteen-year age gap, about the motives they harboured; whether their union was one of convenience and publicity, whether it would last.

All noise.

They didn't care to listen. Lovers rarely do. All they knew was that in finding each other, they had discovered the other half of themselves. They completed each other's sentences and read plays by Camus and Molière, Cervantes and Vega; discussed politics and the environment; travelled to Bora Bora, swam in the azure waters, and made love on its white sands.

They were inseparable, intertwined, indissoluble. They were one and the same, male and female energies charging each other with a glance, a kiss, a touch. The world had shrunk to just the two of them, but their horizons had expanded well beyond their reach.

Such love, they rhapsodised to each other, was granted only to a blessed few. Such love was as rare as the rarest diamond and far more precious. Such love would transcend lifetimes and galaxies, finding them no matter where they went, ambushing them in every incarnation.

Inés knew she was behaving out of character, like a giddy teenager in the first flush of an infatuation. But she couldn't help herself. For the first time in her life, she allowed herself to believe that love, true love, was possible.

Such love. Such dreams. Such belief in the longevity of human emotions. In the steadfastness of man.

Inés would have still believed, if it weren't for the note delivered anonymously to her dressing room.

It turned out that Miguel was a far greater actor than her.

§▲

"Two minutes," Julia called out from behind the door.

"Yes, I'm ready," Inés responded, viewing herself in the mirror. The rehearsals were nearly done, and opening night was only a week away. She swept her hair away from her face, took a deep breath, and proceeded out of the room.

Julia was hovering outside, holding on to a sheaf of papers.

"How's it going?" Inés asked.

"Yes, good, very good. You're on next. The scene with Don Matias?"

"I know."

Inés stepped onto the stage and faced Rita Tamayo, the actress playing Doña Francisquita, her daughter and the eponymous lead of the *zarzuela* based on Lope de Vega's play *La discreta enamorada*. She knew that beyond the brightly lit stage, somewhere in the darkness of the auditorium, her husband was watching. Miguel was no doubt taking notes on how to fine tune the performance, how to give it a modern edge without losing its classical flavour. Miguel, the genius. Miguel, the liar.

She changed her stance to that of a woman much wider, knowing that the padding applied to her figure would transform her into the rotund Doña Francisca, labouring under the misapprehension of Don Matias' affections.

As Pedro entered the stage with a fake bouquet, he threw her a quick wink. They had known each other for over thirty years, and she loved him as a brother. But she couldn't confide in him. He was indiscreet and apt to spread gossip, particularly if it was salacious. She smiled at him, coquettish, flirty, ridiculous. Everything the part demanded of her.

This comic story of multiple love triangles had Doña Francisquita in love with Fernando, who was infatuated with the actress Aurora, who was the lover of Lorenzo Pérez. Don Matias, Fernando's father, tried to woo Francisquita, but Doña Francisca, her mother, believed it was her he was wooing. After a series of misunderstandings and rigmaroles, the true lovers were united at the end, as the entire cast celebrated by singing *Canción de la Juventud,* an ode to the youthful spirit of Madrid.

A song of youth. How very apt. Here she was, Inés, playing the very kind of part that she despised—an object of mockery, an older woman who thought she might be lucky enough to attract a man to want him to marry her.

Her body was going through the motions, showing her excitement at Don Matias' entry, her belief that it was her he wished to woo, and her shock at discovering that he was interested in her daughter. She went through the motions automatically, her many years of experience making her performance near excellent. But Inés' mind was elsewhere. It was on the note that had arrived five days ago. The note that had said: *Be careful. Your husband is cheating on you.*

Even as her mind had rejected the thought, somewhere within her, a seed of suspicion had taken root. There had never been a suggestion in anything Miguel had said or done that could have been construed as duplicity.

Yet.

Here she was, persuaded to fund an extravagant production, in which she had but a measly role.

"*Cariño*, it will be unexpected. No one has seen you in a role like this. This will show them your range, your talent; your ability to morph into anyone." Miguel had worked on her for days, convincing her that this part would lead to so much more. International acclaim, movies with interesting roles, perhaps even the lead part of Hedda Gabler that had always eluded her.

"But I am a soprano! You want me to sing contralto?" she had asked, searching his face.

"My darling, you are a mezzo-soprano. You could sing anything you like."

"Then why can't I play Francisquita? Actresses older than me have played Bizet's Carmen…"

"But that is not the point. I wish to subvert expectations. Naturally, they will expect me to cast you as Francisquita, and when I don't, when that part goes to a different actress, they will wonder what I'm going to do with you."

"So you'll cast me as her dowdy mother?"

"No, no. You, my dear luminous beauty, will offer the unforeseen bonus of transforming yourself into something unexpected—the female comic."

"They will laugh at me."

"That's where you're wrong. They will laugh *with* you."

In that, he hadn't been wrong. From the initial stunned reaction of the cast members, they had come to love the role she embodied. Indeed, they had congratulated her repeatedly on her comic timing, her perfect flounce as well as her ability to make them forget it was Inés Muñoz on the stage. No one had ever seen her take on such a frivolous role and give it so much bite. Pedro had confided in her that when she was on stage, no one bothered watching Rita Tamayo.

"Why her?" she'd cried out in frustration when Miguel had auditioned Rita for the lead. "You know she's been waiting to topple me for ages."

"That's precisely why, Inés. You can show them once and for all who the bigger talent is. You will decimate her, *querida!*"

On stage, she forgot all that. Francisquita became her beloved daughter, heartbroken by Fernando's rejection, desperate enough to accept his father's advances to make him jealous. Inés had never seen the stage as a battleground. To her, it was a playground, a beach even, where many hands came together to create a sandcastle which was beautiful and admired, then washed away by the waves. Until the next evening, and the next, and the next.

She believed in every fibre of her being that theatre was a collaborative effort. Everyone contributed towards the whole. On stage, Rita Tamayo was not her competitor. On stage, she was her daughter, suffering through unrequited love. And, even while the tone of the production was farcical, the emotions of love, heartbreak and rejection were universal. Inés had tapped into those emotions her entire career. Underneath the perfect flounce lay true hurt, and behind the comic timing lay an understanding of the human heart.

On stage, Rita Tamayo was not her competitor. Off stage, she wasn't that sure.

❧

"You are nothing but an actress!"

The words her father had spat out at her mother with such derision had caused Inés to shrink even further back behind the curtains, scared to declare herself. At nine, she had realised that all was not well in their household. Her father, who treated her with nothing less than kindness, was cold and cutting towards her mother. His love had long evaporated, and all that remained in its place was contempt.

Her mother, who came from a long line of famed thespians, was nervous and jumpy in the house, lost in a marriage that had failed to produce anything of value but for a shy and pretty child. Carmen wished to return to the stage, the only place she had ever truly called home. Her skills as a wife and mother were woefully inadequate. Something her husband was careful to point out with regular cruelty.

Theirs had been a marriage of love. A *coup de foudre*, her Basque father declared to one and all. Love at first sight that fizzled soon after the vows had been taken.

As a young man, Martin had been taken to see a theatre production in Madrid while on a business trip. This was where he had first glimpsed Carmen and been smitten instantly by her delicacy and charm. He had harangued his hosts to get him an introduction, and as they did not wish to displease their young guest, they had pulled enough strings to ensure it happened.

At their first meeting, Martin and Carmen had been too shy to speak. At their second, he had proposed. When he brought his pretty *novia* home to meet his family, they had been appalled to discover that she was an actress. Certainly a woman of loose morals and sketchy character. But Martin had refused to budge, willing to forsake his family if it came to that.

As for Carmen, besotted beyond words by the handsome young man and drowning in his ardour, she had ignored all the signs that indicated how very ill-suited she was to life in the Basque Country. With its own language, its own culinary traditions and a distinctive geographic and cultural landscape, it was as far removed from Madrid as it could get.

In time, it became clear that the marriage was a failure. Yet, to the young Inés who adored both her parents, the thought of them separating was impossible to comprehend. Not even when her mother tried explaining it through her tears. Not even when her father flung a piece of paper in Carmen's face, saying, "It's done."

Inés' early years of playing in the shallows of *Playa de Zarautz* or running barefoot on its golden sands were soon overlaid by the monotony of walking to school in heavy black shoes and a pinafore dress. Everything was alien in Madrid, where her mother had brought her to. From the language to the food to this new life with nannies and governesses, her first few years back in her maternal home were miserable.

Even worse were the rare weekends on which her father visited. Inés missed him and wept bitterly when he left. At seventeen, she insisted on accompanying him back, wanting to return to her childhood home and playground. Once back, she came to two realisations. One, that she had grown into a beautiful girl. And two, that she had outgrown the Basque Country.

In the eight years that she had lived away, she had become more citified than she cared to admit. Her life and future were in Madrid, and much to her father's disappointment and his new wife's evident relief, she chose to return a mere fortnight later.

As for Carmen, while her return to theatre wasn't greeted with the rapture she had expected, she carved out a respectable career for herself, playing several leads during the twenty years she inhabited the stage. She never remarried, partly from the scars left over from her ill-fated union, and partly from the need to explore as many men as life would allow her. A revolving door of lovers ensued, leading to as many rows as moments of affection.

In the shadow of such insalubrious beginnings, Inés vowed to herself silently that she would never let love or marriage complicate her own life. She intended to be successful. She had the looks, the talent, the lineage, and the connections. She would not let a man ruin any of it.

Such vows were bound to be tested. Many rich and successful men wooed her, some single and others not so single. They were willing to buy her the largest diamonds, the sleekest yachts, ensconce her in palatial homes and treat her like a princess. None of which made a dent in her stance.

Only one man came close. A fellow thespian stuck in a loveless marriage. A man so magnetic, with such intense eyes, that girls regularly fainted in his presence.

Inés played the Desdemona to his Othello and struck up a similarly doomed love affair with a man sixteen years her senior. That was the singular time she came close to contemplating what it could be like to be someone's wife, to share snippets of each other's days, to eat all of one's meals together; to talk of a future with children, travel and houses, and to slip into dotage together.

Once the rare Spanish musical run of Shakespeare was done with, her Othello melted away, leaving her with precious few memories and a renewed resolve to never be fooled by men and their words again.

"Is he the right one for you?" her father had asked her when she brought Miguel home to meet him. Perhaps he remembered his own time with Carmen and how adamant he had been.

"You are not worried about the age gap?" her mother had asked, perhaps more worried than Inés even. Carmen had always assumed that Inés, her smart, beautiful and powerful daughter, would not make the same mistakes as her.

Now these questions circled in her mind like vultures. Had she rushed into it with her eyes closed? Had all her years of experience, her parents' past, her short-lived infatuation with the institution of marriage and subsequent disillusionment taught her nothing?

Had she married in haste only to repent at leisure?

※

Suspicion is a poisoned chalice. A mere taste is enough for its venom to spread through the entire body. Every look Miguel cast at another woman, every interaction, every throwaway comment, became grist for doubt.

Inés had prided herself on being someone so confident, so secure in herself, that she would never succumb to the pettiness of jealousy. Yet here she was, looking at Miguel with that very lens she had decried on other women.

On the outside, she carried on as normal. Years of acting had given her an armour not even the raging storm inside her would allow to crack. But at some level, she felt she was sleepwalking through life. These weeks which should have been enjoyable, where she no longer carried the burden of the production on her slim shoulders, where she could simply be, were overcast by the gloom of the many vicious thoughts that centred around how she could have been betrayed by a man she had married less than two years ago.

As she looked at herself in the mirror, she noticed the crow's feet at her eyes, the slackening of her jowls, the odd chin hair that had sprung out of nowhere. Is this what Miguel saw every morning when he looked at her? Is this what he regretted sleeping next to? And if so, could she blame him for looking elsewhere?

No!

She pulled herself up. She was Inés Muñoz, *Dama* of the Spanish theatre, darling of the masses. She would not allow herself to be reduced to a sad footnote in some man's life. However brilliant that man was.

Later, much later, when she thought back to the events of those weeks, she wondered why she hadn't confronted Miguel. Why hadn't she simply asked him, caught him unaware when he was busy working out where to use the gobo? Perhaps in that moment she could have fathomed whether he was truly loyal or a lying, treacherous toad.

As it was, she bore her misgivings alone, stewing internally, while externally she paraded as Doña Francisca, the sadly comical mother of the heroine.

She marvelled at the parallels. Were people sniggering behind their hands, wondering how foolish she was to have invested her trust and money in a man she barely knew? Were they all in the know, leaving only her in the dark? Was she unwittingly bringing alive her role in *La Dolorosa*? A jilted woman who was clueless and likely to be abandoned? Had someone felt sorry enough to send her that missive, or was it just a ruse to watch her reaction? To watch her combust at this very public debacle of their connubiality?

At home, Miguel chatted as he prepared the dinner. It was his way to unwind, he'd told her. Cooking relaxed him.

She had taken it as another sign that they were meant to be. She loathed entering the kitchen, had never been interested in food, and often went to bed having eaten just sardines on toast. With Miguel she got used to gourmet dinners washed down with multiple glasses of Rioja.

Inés nursed a glass as she watched him slice the potatoes for the tortilla while the onions sizzled in the pan.

"Can I do something?" she asked, deeply reluctant to move from her position on the sofa.

He looked up at her and grinned, devilishly handsome in the striped apron he had put on. "*Mi amor*, you take it easy. It's been a busy week for you."

"And you." She said it automatically, watching him whisk the eggs.

"Ah yes, but I think it's coming together well. This one will be better than *La Dolorosa*, and that was a triumph, don't you agree?"

"Mmmm." She sipped her wine, eyes on him.

"You," he looked up to meet her eyes, "are everything I imagined you would be."

"Sad, old, fat?" she asked, an edge to her voice.

"No," he seemed not to notice as he carried on stirring the potatoes into the onions, "fantastic, funny, a revelation!"

"And Rita?"

"She is very good, too."

"Better than me?"

Now he paused.

"What is this, Inés?"

"Nothing," she laughed airily, dissipating the tension. "I just wondered if she had lived up to your expectations as well?"

He took a moment before answering.

"The entire cast is excellent, and Rita shows a lot of promise. But you, *querida,* are a class apart."

"You flatter me."

"I tell the truth."

And that, somehow, made her feel even worse.

Going over the months they had spent together, she could not envisage any time that Miguel could have had to indulge in an affair. They had spent every waking moment together, from the beginnings of *La Dolorosa* to their honeymoon and cohabitation in her large flat in Salamanca. They had birthed the idea of *Doña Francisquita* in bed together, giddy from the success of the previous *zarzuela*. She had suggested investing in it, wanting to be a bystander for once, until Miguel had convinced her to take a part. None of his actions were those of a man intent on betraying his wife.

But she had grown up treading the boards, and knew of enough men who hid their mistresses in plain sight. Who had boltholes they escaped to, away from their trusting wives. What guarantee was there that Miguel wasn't one of them? Still, in all the time they had spent together, they had been apart for only a handful of days. Surely not enough time to conduct an affair?

Therefore, there was only one likely suspect. The woman who interacted with Miguel day in, day out—Rita Tamayo.

Rita, of the slanted eyes and sulky mouth; with an hourglass figure that had men salivating at her sight. How easy it would be for someone like Miguel to fall for his dusky protégée. How easy to make love under the guise of giving direction. How easy to trace a finger down an arm unobtrusively, undetectably.

Was Rita's barely concealed envy of Inés camouflaging something far greater? The jealousy and discontent of a love rival?

※

"You are not yourself, Inés," Pedro noted, while taking a large bite out of his apple.

They were between scenes, neither of them required for a while. So, they were sitting together, relaxing and talking about old friends and old times.

"Why do you say that?" Inés sat up, the shawl slipping off her shoulders.

"Quieter than usual." He wiped a bit of juice off his chin with a tissue.

"I have a lot on my mind."

"Such as?"

"Such as… I hope this *zarzuela* does well. I have invested in it, you know."

"Oh, it most certainly will. There is an appetite for it now, and your husband created it." He grinned, taking another bite, and putting his legs up on the velvet footstool. "Already there is talk in the press circles about this grand production. You have nothing to worry about, I assure you!"

"Mmmm."

"But no, it is something else." He looked at her. "You can tell me."

Inés was loath to confide in him, but perhaps if she kept it vague…

"I was wondering about the nature of love."

"Go on."

"How love happens, how it changes, why some loves survive and others… don't."

"Then you are speaking to the expert in these matters." Pedro set aside the apple core and wiped his hands on the tissue.

"Oh?"

"You know how many failed love affairs I have behind me."

Inés was aware of his chequered past.

"But I thought you were happy with…" She'd forgotten the name of his latest paramour.

"José? Ah, he was a *bastardo*," Pedro shrugged in dismissal.

"Then tell me, Don Matias, what do you think of my questions?"

"Love is only a chemical reaction in the brain, and of course, it is not meant to last. Now, whether this love changes into affection and companionship, or whether it turns into enmity and hatred, it is up to the people involved, no?"

"So you think all love stories are doomed?"

"Doomed? No. But happily ever afters do not exist."

"That is very cynical."

Pedro raised his eyebrows and smiled.

"I'd like to think of it as being pragmatic. One is only apt to get disappointed expecting the alternative."

"Hmmm."

Inés replaced the shawl on her shoulders and leaned back into her chair.

"Tell me, *princesa*, is there trouble in paradise?"

Inés closed her eyes to avoid meeting his.

"No, no trouble. Sometimes, though, I cannot help but wonder how a woman of my age can sustain a younger man's interest."

Pedro laughed, and her eyes snapped open.

"What?"

"A woman like you need never wonder that." Pedro took her hand in his. "He is lucky to have you. Do not forget it!"

"Pedro, you are a dear friend and therefore biased."

"Look at me, Inés. I am old—nearly sixty. I have a potbelly and I am balding. But when I look at myself in the mirror, you know what I see? I see a man in the prime of his life. And because I see myself that way, the world sees me that way, too."

Pedro stood up and walked towards the mirror. He adjusted his cravat.

"You are a beautiful woman, but more than that, you are an accomplished one. A beautiful, talented, successful woman. You have financial security, which is more than most women can boast of. And even if everything went wrong with this production and your marriage," he turned around and looked her straight in the eye, "you would still be alright. You could survive anything, and you have to believe that."

A tear slipped out and trickled down her cheek.

"Thank you, Pedro."

"Listen, *chica*, we are all complete in ourselves. No one needs anyone so much that they lose their peace of mind. So, stop worrying about trivial matters and focus on being happy today. After all, that's all we really have, no?"

Maybe she had misjudged Pedro. Besides being an inveterate gossip, he was also a wise old fool who ignored his own advice constantly, falling in and out of love like a feckless teenage boy. Her friend of many years, her early years' partner in mischief and mayhem, her later years' drinking buddy, his words of sagacity were not lost on her.

Miguel walked in on them.

"Well, well. Am I missing out on some juicy anecdotes?"

"We are discussing life and love, matters too serious for a pup like you." Pedro smirked at him.

"You are leading my wife astray."

"I believe you did that already, Señor Miguel. Do you realise how many hearts she broke deciding to settle down with an upstart like you?"

"Well, if these so-called suitors had had the balls, they would have whisked her off well before I came on the scene…"

She watched the two men banter over her and smiled to herself.

Why was she letting the spite of an anonymous note sender destroy everything precious to her? There was no evidence that Miguel had been unfaithful. Would she rather set store by a few words written on a scrap of paper, or believe what her own eyes were seeing?

※

Doubt and suspicion have other friends too. Primary among them is jealousy. Inés thought she had put her strange thoughts to bed, but at the very sight of Rita Tamayo, they reared their heads again.

Rita was in her late twenties, tough as nails, with the ability to go from zero to hundred in a nanosecond. From all accounts she had emerged out of nowhere and taken the theatre world by storm with her very first performance. Rita's personality was as large and loud as the eccentric colour combinations she wore. Unlike Inés, who had always prided herself on looking impeccably elegant, Rita often looked like she had run out of her house, half-dressed and in disarray. But this very chaotic quality gave her an inexplicable edge over her contemporaries.

When it came to the roles she chose, no one could predict what she would do next. She played comedienne and tragedienne with equal ease. When she auditioned for *Doña Francisquita*, she sang the arias with the comfort of a seasoned soprano, and there was no doubt she would bring to the part all the coquettish charm it required.

Even Inés had to acknowledge that the girl had talent.

From the very beginning, though, Rita was prickly with her. There was no respect for a senior actress, no awe, no grovelling or approval-seeking that Inés was accustomed to from anyone who first came into her presence. Wasn't she a legend? And this chit of a girl, who rolled her eyes every time someone said something complimentary about Inés, was arrogant in her disregard and disrespect.

Around Miguel, however, she transformed into a willing student, following him with the sort of slant-eyed devotion that was hard to miss. Inés had met other women like her in the course of her career. Rita Tamayo was a man's woman. Women were competition, men were facilitators. Rita was in a hurry to climb to the top, and she didn't care who she stomped over or who she sucked up to to get there.

When Carmen came to stay two days before opening night, remarking how sorry she was to have missed *La Dolorosa*'s premiere, she said upon her first sighting of Rita Tamayo, "Oh, this one is like Elena Morales."

"Who?" Inés asked while applying false lashes. Her makeup was also caricaturish, much like her character.

Carmen had been taken by surprise that her daughter had chosen to play second fiddle to Rita, remarking, "Look what love reduces us women to."

Now, in the dressing room with her, after watching Rita pretend to love Fernando's father, she said, "Elena Morales was one of my contemporaries. Also beautiful, also fiery. But completely incapable of making friends with another woman. She only surrounded herself with men. Men who would do anything for her, and she made them do plenty!"

"What happened to her?"

"She went to Hollywood, appeared in a few films, did not succeed. Then she married a Greek tycoon and now lives in Beverly Hills somewhere."

"Why does Rita remind you of her?"

"Ambition. Elena never let anything or anyone stand in her way. This one won't, either." She nodded her head sagely.

"Mamá, what does love mean to you?" Inés turned and looked at her diminutive mother in her salmon pink dress and pearl necklace. At seventy-five, she looked ten years younger. Age had been kind to her, and Inés hoped that she too had inherited those genes.

"What a question! Why do you ask this?"

"I'm just curious. After Papá, you never married, but you had love affairs. I know. I was there. And now, you have been with Eduardo for nearly six years. Surely, you have some experience of love?"

"So do you, Inés. Before Miguel, there were many lovers, as I recall."

"Yes, but I'm asking you."

"Well," Carmen sighed and touched her pearls lightly, "before Martin, all my notions of love were silly and romantic. After Martin, I almost gave up on love. Now, I believe that love is what you want it to be. For me, love is a man who will bring me breakfast in bed, help me plant flowers in the garden and take long walks in the rain by my side. Small things that add up to something bigger."

"Hmmm."

"Why? Has Miguel not been kind to you?"

"No, not at all. He has been more than kind. He is loving and supportive, and even this role… It was he who encouraged me to try something different. And you know what, Mamá? I've surprised myself by how much I'm enjoying it."

She beamed at her mother, realising that yes, this was true!

"But there is something…" Carmen asked, perceptive as only a mother could be.

"Yes." Inés turned around to the mirror to finish applying the rest of her makeup. "There is Rita Tamayo. I don't trust her. I feel she is trying to get to Miguel, trying to steal him away from me."

"Elena did that."

"What do you mean?"

"She saw other women's husbands as a challenge. Stealing them was a hobby for her."

"So you think I need to be careful?"

"Oh, one always needs to be careful, especially when you are at a disadvantage."

"Such as?"

"The age, my dear one. You cannot ignore *la mierda bajo la alfombra!*"

For a while she had forgotten, but now, with her mother's reminder, all her old insecurities rose to the surface. There was no denying the nearly two decade difference between Miguel and her. He had never commented upon it, except at the very beginning when she had brought it up.

"These things do not matter to me, Inés. I am in love with the essence of you, not what is on the outside."

And of course, that had only made her fall even more deeply in love with her dashing swain.

Now, she wondered if after so many months of wedded bliss; he was still captivated by her essence, or whether the lure of another, perhaps younger, woman had proven to be irresistible.

※

Opening night was always fraught with tension. Regardless of how prepared the cast was, how favourable the advance reviews had been, there was always the danger that the audience would hate the production; that word would spread that it was sub-par and that ticket sales would plummet, leading them to fold early.

From the opening market scene where Fernando had gone to admire Aurora (played by the wonderfully versatile Cora Isaura, who was a lovely lady in reality but played negative parts extremely well), Inés knew that the audience was captivated. Miguel had spared no expense in creating the extraordinary sets that replicated Madrid during the Carnival season in the 19th century. Their costumes were equally rich—velvets, satins and silks in jewel tones, *mantillas* adorning the *peinetas* in their hair. The women were beautiful, the men dashing, the music thrilling, emotional and sensuous. The orchestra was led by none other than the renowned Juan Carlos

Lascala; the notes soaring and dipping like winged birds in euphoric flight.

There were nerves, but they only added to the anticipation of performing in front of a live audience. The entire cast had held hands before the performance, trying to communicate confidence, vigour and luck to one another.

Just before entering the stage, Inés had looked at Rita and said, "*Mucha Mierda*. Break a leg, Rita. I'm sure you will be wonderful."

In response, Rita had raised her brows, given her an insouciant grin, and marched ahead to the stage. She realised at that moment that no matter how kind or gracious she was to Rita; it was not likely to be reciprocated. A consummate professional, Inés had plastered a smile on her face and waddled in behind her.

At the end of Act 1, it was clear that while everyone was doing a remarkable job; it was her, Inés, in the role of Doña Francisca, who was getting the loudest cheers.

"What is happening?" She touched her cheeks backstage, hot and reddened under the lights.

"They are loving you! It is as Miguel had predicted," Pedro laughed, yanking at her *mantilla*.

"*Oh querido*! Rita will not like this."

"What do you care, *chica*? In the end, it is the *zarzuela* that has to succeed, and if your performance brings in the crowds, then so be it!"

"Pedro?"

"Yes?"

"There was a note…"

But before she could say any more, Act 2 had begun, and they were back on stage.

While performing, it was easy to forget that there was another world out there. In that moment, she was Doña Francisca, the ludicrous older woman in search of love. As the multiple strands of love machinations played out around her, Inés threw herself into her role, inviting both ridicule for the character's hapless behaviour and praise for the way she inhabited her.

By Act 3, she was enjoying herself tremendously. It no longer mattered that she wasn't the lead. Even Cora had a meatier role than her, but after many, many years, she had gotten the chance to explore her comedic side. To relax into a role that demanded something different from her.

Now and again, real life would intrude in a hastily given instruction backstage, or a sip of Coca Cola, a wink from Pedro, a smile from Cora, or a venomous glance from Rita.

All evening she had felt waves of loathing emanate from her person, and as the performance progressed, she realised it wasn't in her imagination. Rita was giving a perfectly competent performance. Some might have even said an excellent one, but there were undercurrents of animosity that swirled around Inés, disturbing her, throwing her off at times. Rita Tamayo was declaring war in the most undetectable manner.

What was this if not a love rivalry? Inés had never pretended to be a friend, but equally she had never shown an overt dislike towards Rita. This resentment, this anger, was unwarranted unless something far more sinister lay at the heart of it. Perhaps a desire to depose an adversary?

It wasn't until the final act that Rita's simmering jealousy came to a head. Even as they were singing and dancing to the last *fandango*, twirling and spinning, clacking *castanets*, changing partners as they danced, she hissed into Inés' ear, "He only married you for your money," before skipping away with another partner.

Curtain call after curtain call, the rapturous applause told them they had a triumph on their hands. It would be called a *tour de force* in the days to come, each cast member getting multiple write ups on their performances. Rita Tamayo would be hailed as 'delightful', Cora Isaura as 'mesmerising', Pedro as 'a master at work' and Inés as the 'biggest revelation of the night'. Miguel would be 'an undeniable wizard', with the ability to transcend the source material and create an altogether unforgettable, magical experience for theatre-goers. The *zarzuela* would become the performance of choice for Spanish audiences in the years to come.

Curtain call after curtain call, Inés smiled till her cheeks hurt, her eyes glittering, her skin aglow. Inside her, a shard of ice had lodged itself in her heart, a cold hard certainty taking root. When had love ever delivered happiness? Only in *zarzuelas* did everyone find a happy ending. In real life, all you found was the rottenness of deception. But she smiled and blew kisses and no one would have known that anything was amiss.

It was four in the morning when they returned home. She had been quiet in the car, and Miguel had assumed it was fatigue. He was too wired to notice anything else, going over the entire evening in minute detail, not waiting for a response, jumping from one topic to another, triumphant, ecstatic, vindicated.

At home, he poured them each a glass of wine and sat beside her on the sofa.

"Are you happy, *corazón*?" He put one arm behind her, drawing slow circles on her shoulder while sipping on his wine.

"How long, Miguel?"

"Eh?"

"How long has it been going on?"

He stiffened and moved away, turning to stare at her.

"How long has what been going on?"

"Don't mock me!"

He placed his glass on the table and turned his entire body towards her.

"You need to explain yourself more clearly, Inés." His eyes were as cold as his voice, and she shivered in response.

"You and Rita."

"Me and Rita, what?"

"Your affair!"

"Our what?"

Inés stood up and walked towards the window.

"Whatever you do, Miguel, do not lie to me. I am too old and too tired for silly games." She turned around to face him, taking a few steps then stopping, her eyes searching his, waiting for him to deny, to deflect, to tell her she was crazy and had an overactive imagination. Everything men did to women, every day. Women they wished to gaslight into submission.

He gave a short, abrupt laugh, then stood up and came towards her. "You think I've been having an affair with Rita Tamayo?"

She nodded, drawing herself up to her full height. Feeling wretched and lonely, then suddenly feeling enraged on behalf of all betrayed women.

"And what makes you think this?" He ran his hands through his hair, eyes narrowed, watching her closely.

"There was a note, an anonymous one, that warned me to be careful. And then, today, on the stage, she told me… she said that you had only married me for my money."

He drew in a deep breath and went to stand by the window. A few moments later, he said, "Do you remember when you'd asked me what love meant to me?"

She did.

She'd asked him that question while they'd lain in side-by-side hammocks on a sun-kissed island in the Caribbean, their fingers interlaced. He'd laughed and given her a frivolous response, and she'd laughed too, then forgotten all about it.

Now he turned to face her, his eyes sad, "Love means trust, Inés. It is the foundation of everything. Do you trust me?"

She shook her head. "Trust yes, not blind faith."

"Do you trust me?" he asked again.

"Miguel…"

"No," he raised his hand to stop her, "I want to know. How long have you been suspecting me?"

She cleared her throat. "A few weeks."

"A few weeks in which you have thought that I have been unfaithful and you haven't asked me a single question. Weeks where you have gone to bed believing me to be a liar!"

"Yes."

"Okay, tell me why. Why would I do this to you?"

"Because! Look at me and look at you. Look at our age gap."

"Back to that again? When are you going to understand that it makes no difference to me? What if it were the other way round? What if I was twenty years older than you?"

"It wouldn't matter. You are a man."

He laughed again, a short, sharp bark.

"Listen to yourself, Inés. This isn't you talking. This is years and years of conditioning. Society has taught you that what is acceptable for a man isn't acceptable for a woman. This life and this profession have taught you that men are cheats and women are fools, and that is the only narrative that is valid. You have taken these lessons and turned them into your truths."

"Perhaps," she answered as coldly as he had before. "But my instincts have never betrayed me. And if age is not a factor, boredom is. Men are fickle and treacherous. I had hoped you weren't, but now…"

Miguel glanced at her, his brow furrowed.

"Did you ever consider that whoever sent you that note might have been lying? That it was coming from a place of jealousy and unhappiness, that it was meant to prey on all your insecurities and turn you into a nervous wreck just before opening night?"

"Who would do that?"

He shrugged.

"The obvious suspect is Rita, but it really doesn't matter. What matters is that you didn't trust me enough to ask me yourself."

"I asked you today."

"Only after having made up your mind about it, about me. And the answer, Inés, is no. No, I am not having an affair with Rita Tamayo. There had once been a brief liaison between us, many years ago. But that fizzled out and right now I have no interest in Rita Tamayo, aside from the fact that she is my lead actress. It is you I married, because it was you I fell in love with. If someone had come to me with an accusation against you, it is *you* I would have asked first."

She turned her back on him, digesting the news silently.

"Are you going to hold my past against me, Inés? Are you going to destroy us over something as ridiculous as that?"

She remained silent. Miguel came and stood next to her, looking out of the window with her.

"Can I ask you a question?"

She nodded.

"Do you want us to last?"

Did she?

She turned towards him, her face betraying none of the turmoil inside her. Did she want a future with Miguel? A happy, secure future?

"Inés, no one can guarantee lasting happiness," he said, as if reading her mind. "There may come a day when you weary of me or I of you. There may come a day when one of us gets sick and dies. There may come a day when we mutually decide to separate because this relationship does not satisfy us anymore." He put a finger under her chin and lifted it gently. "But today is not that day if you don't let it be."

She watched him carefully, assessing his words, assessing him.

Miguel took her hand in his, turned her palm up, and placed a kiss on it. "In return," he said, "all I ask of you is to be kind to us and to believe in us. Believe that we are possible and good together. Can you do that?"

Inés thought back to the two years she had spent with him. The months of love, companionship and laughter they had shared. Of the strange synchronicity that existed between them. Had she really been willing to throw it all away over an anonymous note and a jilted, jealous rival?

Miguel stood there, waiting for a response, his face a picture of misery.

Inés nodded, moving closer until she had settled herself into the crook of his arm, her body melding to his, forgiveness coming as instinctively as the realisation that the only person responsible for her happiness was herself.

She believed Miguel, not because of his words, words could lie, but because of the way he clasped her hand, the way hope replaced the sadness in his eyes, and the slight trembling of his body as he held her close. This was a man fearful of losing his love, not a man scared of being found out. She knew enough to know that this was true.

Pedro had called love a chemical reaction, Mamá had claimed it was companionship, and for Miguel it was trust. But what was love to her? An all-consuming passion or a deep sense of comfort and security?

All her life she had watched relationships implode, she had watched them disintegrate. She had seen betrayal and deception; she had been subjected to rancour and fury. Had she automatically put an expiry date on all love, especially her own? Had she led with fear instead of conviction?

What did love mean to her?

She had yet to define it like the others, and perhaps she would spend the rest of her life trying to understand it. Yet these last few weeks had shown her that love needed courage rather than cowardice, belief rather than mistrust. Yes, understanding love would be a life-long pursuit for her, and she hoped that she and Miguel could do it together. And even if they didn't, did it really matter? Whether love was fragile or enduring, long or short-lived, all that mattered was that she had experienced it.

In this present moment, however, love meant the simple oblivion of her husband's embrace, the soft kiss he planted on her head, and the realisation that this was a benediction granted only to the most fortunate.

Ámame cuando menos lo merezca, porque será cuando más lo necesite.

(Love me when I least deserve it, because it will be when I need it the most.)

SIX - STRANGE STORIES OF LOVE

THE END

Did you enjoy this book? Would you like to read the other two in the collection?

Twelve - stories from around the world
Eight - Fantastical Tales From Here, There & Everywhere

AFTERWORD

Word-of-mouth is crucial for any author to succeed and if you found this book interesting please do leave a review on your preferred retailer. Even if it's just a star rating or a sentence or two, it would make all the difference and would be very much appreciated!

If you enjoyed this book, you can sign up to hear more about my new releases and any special offers!

Do visit www.poornimamanco.com to keep abreast of all my news.

ACKNOWLEDGMENTS

This is where I'm nearly always stumped for words. Who do I thank? Where do I begin? There are so many people who have brought love and joy into my life that putting all their names down would be an impossible task.

I have dedicated this book to my family, so I'll begin there.

Mike, thank you for your patience with my impossible hours and bizarre sleep patterns while working on this book. Prianka, thank you for being my alpha reader, for providing me with feedback, ideas and insights that only someone of your age and intelligence would have. Mahika, thank you for the many long chats we've had about people, psyches and motivations. I'm always amazed by your wisdom. I love you, family, and realise how incredibly lucky I am to have you in my life.

To all the people who helped me with authenticity in language and location in these many tales, deep and heartfelt gratitude. Chuck, Avril, Veronica, Susannah, Christian and Monica, these stories would not have been possible without your input.

To my beta and advance readers (Paul, Valerie, An, Mireille, Samantha, Maria, Vibha and Sacha), thank you for your time, support and encouragement. Your honest reviews help me hone my craft, and I hope with each new book you find that I have improved just a wee bit more. An extra special shout-out to Roshni, another of my advance readers, who also became my sounding board and voice of reason and wisdom, guiding me towards a better connection with my readers.

Thank you to my editor par excellence, Charulatha Dasappa.

Without you, none of this would be possible. To Team MiblArt for bringing my vision of the cover to life. Your multiple iterations until you hit upon the 'right one' are very, very appreciated.

Finally, thank you to you readers for your trust and your patronage. I hope that I can continue to entertain you for many years to come.

ABOUT THE AUTHOR

Author of six short story collections, one novella and two novels, Poornima has lived more than half her life outside of India, her birthplace. Still, you can take the girl out of India, but you cannot take India out of the girl. Nearly all her books and stories show the deep connection she retains to her motherland.

Poornima lives in the United Kingdom with her family.

ALSO BY POORNIMA MANCO

Parvathy's Well & other stories

Damage & other stories

Holi Moly! & other stories

The Intimacy of Loss

Twelve - stories from around the world

Parvathy's Well & Other Stories: The India Collection

Eight - Fantastical Tales From Here, There & Everywhere

Six - Strange Stories of Love

A Quiet Dissonance

Intersections - A Novel

Printed in Great Britain
by Amazon